AFTERWORD

I'm sorry to have kept you waiting for so long! Thank you for reading Volume 4 of *The Isolator*!

The previous volume came out in February 2016, so this is the first new book in a year and three months. As if that weren't long enough, from the perspective of those readers following along in real time on the web version, they've been waiting for the continuation of part three for eight years now... And since I was continuing a story that I left off eight years ago, it was naturally rather difficult to remember what ideas I had at the time. In the beginning, my no-planning method totally backfired, to the point where I thought I would have to come up with a new story entirely because I couldn't remember anything... But strangely enough, as I started writing, it felt as if my characters were telling me, "This part was supposed to go like this!" So I think I may have managed to stay fairly close to the original plan.

On the other hand, since scientific knowledge has been updated so much in the past eight years, it was hard to bring things up to date. For instance, in this volume, the Third Eye's power to manipulate molecules is called the "seventh force," but it was originally going to be the "fifth force." Why fifth? Because of what's known as the "four fundamental forces" that work between elementary particles: weak forces, strong forces, electromagnetic forces, and gravitational forces. To sum it up, weak forces are carried by elementary particles called weak bosons, strong forces are controlled by gluons, electromagnetic forces are what make giant robots move and stuff, and gravity is what makes them fall when they're defeated in battle.

So, eight years ago, I thought I would call the Third Eye's ability to manipulate molecules (elementary particles) the fifth force... But when I did a little research as I was starting to write this book, I found out that a fifth force had been discovered just last year! (It's the intermediary between protophobic and boson particles...so cool...) And then there were more essays that said things like "There might be a sixth force, too?!" so I figured I'd just have to make it the seventh one instead! That's why it became the seventh force. There will probably be more problems like that in the future, but I hope you'll still continue to cheer on our heroes, as Minoru grows little by little and Yumiko starts to soften a bit.

Finally, I'd like to once again thank Shimeji for drawing such beautiful, impressive illustrations this volume! I'm so sorry to you and Miki for how last-minute everything ended up being! I'll do my best for Volume 5, so I hope you'll continue to support me!

A certain day in April 2017
Reki Kawahara

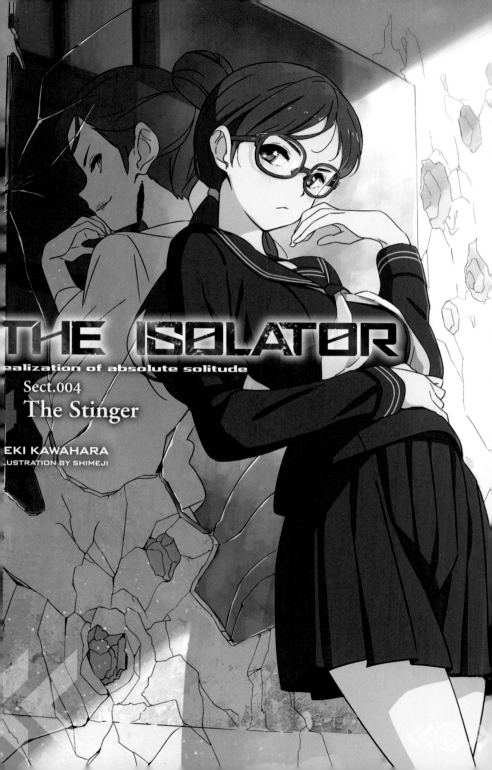

THE ISOLATOR

realization of absolute solitude

Sect.004
The Stinger

REKI KAWAHARA
ILLUSTRATION BY SHIMEJI

"......"

» SUU KOMURA
THE MEMBER WITH THE MOST POWERFUL
ABILITY IN THE JET EYE ORGANIZATION, THE
SFD. SHE SUFFERED SERIOUS INJURIES IN
THE FIGHT AGAINST THE SYNDICATE THAT
HAVE RENDERED HER UNCONSCIOUS. HER
CODE NAME IS REFRACTOR. SHE HAS THE
ABILITY TO BECOME INVISIBLE.

TOMOMI MINOWA

A HIGH SCHOOL GIRL WHO'S BEEN CLASSMATES WITH MINORU SINCE MIDDLE SCHOOL. WHEN SHE LOST HER MEMORIES OF BEING ATTACKED BY BITER, SHE ALSO FORGOT HER FRIENDSHIP WITH MINORU, BUT THEY ENDED UP BECOMING FRIENDS AGAIN.

"HEE-HEE, THANKS."

"DON'T COME ANY CLOSER, PLEASE."

▶▶ TRANCER
A YOUNG RUBY EYE WHO GOES
BY RYUU MIKAWA. USED TO BE
LIQUIDIZER'S APPRENTICE. HE
HAS THE ABILITY TO FREEZE
WATER INSTANTLY.

"HMM.
SO THIS IS
YOUR LITTLE
NEST, IS IT,
BOY?"

≫ LIQUIDZER

THE STRONGEST MEMBER OF THE RUBY
EYE ORGANIZATION, THE SYNDICATE. SHE
SOMETIMES APPEARS AS A CAREER WOMAN
AND SOMETIMES AS A HIGH SCHOOL GIRL
IN A SAILOR UNIFORM. SHE HAS THE ABILITY
TO LIQUEFY SOLID MATTER.

"_____"

STINGER

A RUBY EYE WHOSE NAME AND
MOTIVES ARE UNKNOWN. ABLE TO
MANIPULATE VARIOUS ABILITIES,
AND TARGETS MEMBERS OF THE
SYNDICATE AS WELL AS THE SFD.

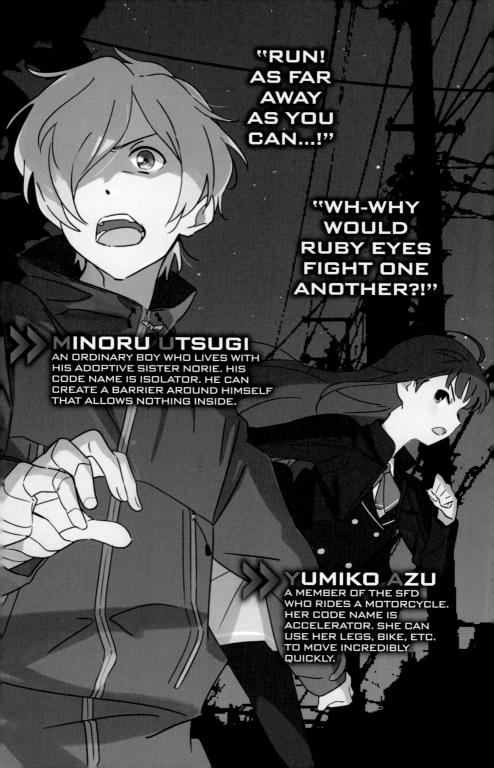

"RUN! AS FAR AWAY AS YOU CAN...!"

"WH-WHY WOULD RUBY EYES FIGHT ONE ANOTHER?!"

MINORU UTSUGI
AN ORDINARY BOY WHO LIVES WITH HIS ADOPTIVE SISTER NORIE. HIS CODE NAME IS ISOLATOR. HE CAN CREATE A BARRIER AROUND HIMSELF THAT ALLOWS NOTHING INSIDE.

YUMIKO AZU
A MEMBER OF THE SFD WHO RIDES A MOTORCYCLE. HER CODE NAME IS ACCELERATOR. SHE CAN USE HER LEGS, BIKE, ETC. TO MOVE INCREDIBLY QUICKLY.

THE ISOLATOR
realization of absolute solitude 《◎》 CONTENTS

THE ISOLATOR
realization of absolute solitude

Sect. 004 The Stinger

"I'M LOOKING FOR ABSOLUTE SOLITUDE... THAT'S WHY MY CODE NAME IS ISOLATOR."

REKI KAWAHARA
ILLUSTRATIONS BY SHIMEJI

YEN ON

NEW YORK

THE ISOLATOR Volume 4
© REKI KAWAHARA

Translation by Jenny McKeon
Cover art by Shimeji

ZETTAI NARU ISOLATOR Vol.4
©REKI KAWAHARA 2017
Edited by ASCII MEDIA WORKS
First published in Japan in 2017 by KADOKAWA CORPORATION, Tokyo.
English translation rights arranged with KADOKAWA CORPORATION, Tokyo, through TUTTLE-MORI
AGENCY, INC.

English translation © 2018 by Yen Press, LLC

Yen On
1290 Avenue of the Americas
New York, NY 10104

Visit us at yenpress.com
facebook.com/yenpress
twitter.com/yenpress
yenpress.tumblr.com
instagram.com/yenpress

First Yen On Edition: May 2018

Yen On is an imprint of Yen Press, LLC.
The Yen On name and logo are trademarks of Yen Press, LLC.

Library of Congress Cataloging-in-Publication Data

Names: Kawahara, Reki, author. | Shimeji, illustrator. | Trask, Adair, translator. |
    ZephyrRz, translator. | McKeon, Jenny, translator.
Title: The Isolator, realization of absolute solitude. / Reki Kawahara ;
    illustrations by Shimeji ; translation by Jenny McKeon.
Other titles: Zettai naru Isolator. English
Description: First Yen On edition. | New York, NY : Yen On, 2015– |
    v. 3–4 translation by Jenny McKeon.
Identifiers: LCCN 2015034584 | ISBN 9780316260596 (v. 1 : hardback) |
    ISBN 9780316268899 (v. 2 : hardback) | ISBN 9780316552721
    (v. 3 : hardback) | ISBN 9781975326272 (v. 4 : hardback)
Subjects: | CYAC: Orphans—Fiction. | Solitude—Fiction. | Science fiction. |
    BISAC: FICTION / Science Fiction / Adventure.
Classification: LCC PZ7.K1755 It 2016 | DDC [Fic]—dc23
LC record available at https://lccn.loc.gov/2015034584

ISBNs: 978-1-9753-2627-2 (hardcover)
    978-1-9753-2684-5 (ebook)

1 3 5 7 9 10 8 6 4 2

LSC-C

Printed in the United States of America

Early morning in midwinter. The temperature was just above zero.

Even with a face mask, the air was so cold that it stabbed at his lungs.

The asphalt glittered with flecks of frost as he crossed it in long strides. The shaking motion reverberated through the cast on his arm, but the pain wasn't too intense anymore.

The morning mist clinging to the promenade on the bank shone crimson in the light of dawn.

Beyond the haze, a set of steady footsteps was approaching.

It was probably a man, judging by the pace and body weight. He seemed strong. He was moving fairly quickly, too, but wasn't very young. In his thirties…no, forties, perhaps.

As he sensed all this just from the sound of the man's footsteps, Minoru shifted to the left-hand side of the cycling road, slowing his speed from sixteen kilometers per hour to ten. After a few seconds, the person's shadow appeared before him. They passed each other in silence.

Just as he'd suspected, it was a male runner in his prime, sporting a thin beard. The athlete was moving at a speed of almost thirteen kilometers per hour. Running at a powerful clip that seemed to carve through the mist, he was soon far behind Minoru, the strong scent of sweat disappearing shortly after.

Returning to his original pace and position, Minoru fell deep into thought.

It was probably quite difficult to maintain such a pace at that age. And considering how much force of will it took for Minoru to drag himself out of bed to go for a run before school, it must be twice as tough to do so before a morning commute to work. Even his adoptive older sister Norie, who was always bright and cheerful, tended to be a bit low energy in the morning. Though since it was January 3, Norie was still sound asleep in bed.

Minoru wanted to keep running when he reached that man's age, too, which was why he had started this morning routine, but three—no, four—months ago, he'd had to admit that his morning runs had lost a bit of their meaning.

The goal of exercise is to exert one's body, so if it isn't at least a little challenging, there isn't much point. It could even be said that what makes exercise enjoyable is withstanding the pain and struggle to push the body's limits.

But now, even if Minoru ran at a speed of twenty kilometers per hour for nine or ten kilometers, he didn't feel short of breath. And twenty kilometers per hour is the average for top-class male marathon runners appearing in the Olympics. If he wanted to put serious strain on his lungs, he'd have to run even faster, but speeding along the bank of the Arakawa River at almost thirty-two kilometers per hour was sure to draw more than just suspicion. And since Minoru was afraid of being remembered by other people, he could never do something like that.

"...I wish I could turn your powers on and off..."

Minoru murmured in a low voice as he ran.

Of course, there was no answer. The sphere, roughly two centimeters around, embedded in his chest—the inky-black "Third Eye"—had no consciousness of its own. It only served to increase the physical abilities of its host and provide that host with a supernatural ability.

Riri Isa, a professor who worked along with Minoru for the Ministry of Health, Labor, and Welfare Industrial Safety and Health Department, Specialized Forces Division (SFD for short), was researching how Third Eyes could give their hosts such abnormal strength, endurance, and so on, but so far, she hadn't made any progress in understanding the parasite's basic structure.

However, as a phenomenon, a few discoveries had been made.

All eukaryotes, including humans, use a substance known as "adenosine triphosphate" as an energy source for cellular activity. Minoru remembered learning about ATP in biology class.

ATP is a molecule composed of three phosphate groups sticking to a nucleoside called adenosine. When one of the phosphate groups detaches, a large amount of energy is generated. The human body uses this energy for tasks like contracting muscles and digesting food particles.

ATP that has lost a phosphate group in this way changes to "adenosine diphosphate," or ADP. Energy obtained from meals is used to attach phosphate to ADP to turn it back into ATP. This cycle is constantly being repeated in the human body.

However, the Professor had discovered an unknown compound among the cells of Minoru and the other Jet Eyes.

Like ATP, it was composed of phosphate groups attached to adenosine. But in this case, there were actually nine phosphates attached.

Professor Riri Isa gave the compound the temporary name "adenosine nonaphosphate," or ANP for short.

ANP could disconnect seven phosphate groups before becoming ADP. In other words, it could generate seven times more energy than that of ATP. The Professor said this was probably one of the reasons that Third Eye holders had higher physical strength and fitness than the average person. At the same time, however, she had no idea how the Third Eyes were producing such a powerful compound.

The Professor herself was a Jet Eye with an ability that allowed her to immediately answer any question as long as it was possible to glean the information from available data, skipping the reasoning process entirely. If even she couldn't understand it, Minoru suspected that the mysteries of the Third Eyes would never be solved. Perhaps the power of these small spheres—and the reason for their existence—stood beyond the scope of human comprehension.

This miraculous parasite known as the Third Eye was far from being all-powerful, though. There was still a limit to its ability to enhance its host's body.

Third Eye hosts couldn't run forever without needing to rest, or lift a car, or anything like that. And if one were flung against solid concrete at full force, they would certainly be seriously injured.

"......Suu..."

Once again, an unintentional mumble escaped Minoru's lips, but there was no answer.

Feeling thirsty, he started slowing down. In front of him, he could make out a bollard on the north side of the Sakitama Bridge. He stopped and took a deep breath. Looking at the special SFD-made running watch on his left wrist, he noticed his slightly elevated heart rate come down immediately.

Before the Third Eye took root in Minoru's body, he hadn't needed to hydrate during his daily six-mile run. But in exchange for raising the host's physical strength, the Third Eye consumed a great deal of fluid and glucose. Of course, if he kept his running speed at the same level as before, the consumption would decrease accordingly, but then it would barely feel like running at all. He'd gotten carried away and averaged around fifteen kilometers per hour, too, so he was already parched at this turnaround point on his route.

Vending machines were mostly absent from the riverbanks of the Arakawa. He could theoretically buy something to drink at Saiko Park on the west side or head over to the residential area on the east side, but either detour would interrupt his running for quite a while.

As a result, Minoru had started wearing another special SFD device under his Windbreaker: a hydration pack. There was a five hundred–milliliter waterproof PPS-film reservoir on the back, which he could drink from with an attached tube. The capacity was rather modest compared with most packs on the market, but it didn't feel as burdensome as a rucksack or waist pouch and had no effect on his free-dom of movement.

Lowering his face mask, Minoru pulled out a thin tube from beneath his collar and popped the valve on the end into his mouth. The water that flowed into his mouth was a bit lukewarm, of course, but he had no complaints. Besides, drinking cold water on a midwinter run would just chill his stomach more.

Leaning on a bollard and sipping on the water warmed by his own body temperature, Minoru looked up at the south sky.

New Year's Eve had been three days ago—December 31, 2019.

Sent on a reconnaissance mission for the SFD, Minoru had infiltrated an unmarked building in Minami-Aoyama, Minato Ward, Tokyo.

It was the location of a safe house for the Jet Eyes' opposition, the Ruby Eye group known as the "Syndicate"...in other words, a hideout. Of course, since the mission was expected to be dangerous, Professor Riri Isa had prepared the best defensive measures that could be mus-tered with the current members of the organization.

Under the code name of Isolator, Minoru had the ability to make a transparent barrier capable of shielding him from any attack, and he could combine it perfectly with Refractor's—Suu Komura's—power of invisibility.

The mechanics of their combination were very primitive, though: Minoru carried Suu on his back while they both invoked their abilities. But at the same time, their combination was nothing short of miracu-lous. Because Suu Komura was the only member of the SFD—the only person in the world, in fact—who Minoru had been able to bring into his shell.

Protected by Minoru's barrier and Suu's invisibility, the two of them entered the safe house in Minami-Aoyama as an invisible, invincible pair. But they fell into a trap set there for them by a presumed executive of the Syndicate, the Ruby Eye who went by the code name Liquidizer.

With the terrifying ability to turn substance into liquid, she had liquefied the concrete that filled the first floor of the safe house, trapping Minoru and Suu inside.

The heavy concrete, which rehardened instantly, wouldn't crack no matter how many times Minoru hit it with his shell. When the two SFD members positioned outside—Denjirou "DD" Daimon and the Accelerator Yumiko Azu—warned them that danger was approaching, Suu attempted to enact a desperate last-ditch measure.

The instant a Jet Eye or Ruby Eye ceases living, it triggers a reaction in the Third Eye located somewhere in their body known as the "exodus" phenomenon.

The Third Eye separates itself from the host and shoots up toward the sky, probably to space, at tremendous speed. There was no way of stopping it. Even if it were surrounded by steel ninety centimeters thick, the Third Eye would open a large hole right through it.

Suu tried to use that supernatural phenomenon. She deliberately ejected herself from Minoru's shell, trying to let herself be crushed to death by the pressure of the concrete and the shell to induce the Third Eye's exodus.

Minoru was able to deactivate his power just in time to prevent Suu's death. However, she sustained serious injuries from flying into the concrete at top speed and was taken away in a comatose state by medevac. She was still currently being treated at the ICU of the hospital in the city center, and Minoru hadn't heard anything about her regaining consciousness.

Minoru planned on visiting Suu for the first time in the early afternoon. He'd asked for permission countless times since the night of the mission, and the Professor had finally granted it.

Of course, even if he went, they wouldn't be able to talk together, and he might not be able to see her at all. But no matter what, he wanted to share his thoughts with her from as close by as possible. He hadn't even thanked her for saving him and the lives of the others, after all.

Removing the water tube from his mouth, he lifted his injured right hand.

A simple fracture of the ulna. An open fracture of the third and fourth metacarpal bones. Avulsion fractures of the ring finger and little finger. Extensive muscle lacerations. It was severe enough that the doctor who treated him furrowed his brow, but compared with most of the other SFD members who participated in the recon mission, Minoru's injuries were minor. In fact, the initial pain was almost gone after just three days.

Yumiko's wounds were limited to the scratches on her legs, but Olivier Saito (the Divider), who'd arrived just in time for the battle with the Trancer, a Ruby Eye, took a direct hit from a hand grenade made of ice and suffered gashes and bruises all over his body. Thanks to his cutting ability and the healing powers of the Third Eye, none of his wounds were fatal; but he was still admitted to the hospital near headquarters, and apparently, it would be a few more days before his release.

Meanwhile, their enemies, known only as Liquidizer and Trancer, seemed to have been seriously wounded as well, but they had escaped by liquefying the ground of the factory that had served as the battlefield, and their whereabouts were unknown. The Japan Self-Defense Forces were supposed to be carrying out a new strategy based on the information Minoru and Suu acquired in the safe house, but there was no news of any results yet.

"...So why...did Suu have to...?"

Muttering in a strangled voice, Minoru tried to clench his still-injured right hand, but the 3-D-printed synthetic was incredibly tough despite the thinness of the material, so he was only able to cause the slightest creak.

With a long sigh, Minoru raised himself off the bollard.

When questioned by his adoptive sister, Norie Yoshimizu, he told her that he'd only fallen and bruised his hand while running, but he couldn't help but feel ashamed at how often he lied to her since joining the SFD. He treasured Norie above anyone else in the world and never wanted to cause her sadness or concern, but the situation seemed to be rapidly going downhill. Three days before the reconnaissance mission, he'd even gone to the Tokyo Bay Nuclear Power Plant, a place full of highly lethal radiation, and entered the housing unit of a nuclear reactor unaided.

Ruby Eyes killed people. Jet Eyes stopped them. Minoru couldn't deny this reality any longer. But if he kept on accumulating secrets like this, Minoru was sure that one day everything would fall apart.

There was only one way to solve this problem.

He would have Chief Himi, the head of the SFD who held the frightening power to manipulate other people's memories, remove all traces of Minoru from Norie's mind. Then he would leave home without a trace and move into SFD Headquarters. That way, no Ruby Eyes would be drawn to the house by Minoru's scent and attack Norie.

But...Minoru didn't want that.

It didn't seem right to manipulate Norie's memories, but more than that, Minoru himself didn't really want to leave his current home. He didn't want to give up his life with Norie. So because of his own ego, he continued to lie to the person he loved most in the world and expose her to danger.

"......"

Heaving another long sigh, Minoru got ready to resume running.

However, right before taking his first step, he noticed the presence of another person again. This time, the footsteps that approached through the thick morning fog were clearly different from those of the man who passed a few minutes earlier.

How strange that this many people would be out running on the Arakawa River so early on the third day of the New Year... As he contemplated this without a hint of irony, Minoru retreated to the side. Keeping his eyes down, he waited for the runner to pass.

Wait... By the time he started to think this, the other person was already calling out to him.

"Ah, it's Utsugi!"

A petite girl in a green Windbreaker slowed her pace as she shouted.

This was no stranger but instead Minoru's schoolmate. She was a first-year at Yoshiki High School just like him and a member of the track-and-field club: Tomomi Minowa.

Minoru had no idea how to respond as she ran up to him.

He and Tomomi had met up five times in the past two weeks to go running together, but today they had no such plans. But a chance encounter like this might make it seem like Minoru had been waiting on the bank to ambush her.

Oblivious to the worries saturating Minoru's mind, Tomomi showed him a carefree smile as she spoke.

"Man, you should've let me know you'd be running today! I figured you were starting tomorrow."

"Oh, um…"

His thoughts still scattered, Minoru straightened his back and spoke.

"Happy New Year, Minowa."

Tomomi blinked for a moment, then quickly flashed another smile and ducked her head.

"You too, Utsugi. Happy New Year! Let's both make it a good one, yeah?"

"Y-yeah, definitely…"

Tomomi seemed to be giggling a little as she looked up toward him, so Minoru couldn't help but ask a question.

"D-did I say something funny…?"

"No, no, not at all. Sorry for laughing."

Her short, bobbed hair swaying as she shook her head, Tomomi smiled again.

"I've just never been given such a polite New Year's greeting by someone my age before."

"…That might've been my first time doing it, too."

"Ah-ha-ha! But it's kind of nice, saying it in person instead of over LANE or whatever."

When Tomomi mentioned the name of a popular messaging app, Minoru couldn't help but nod in agreement.

"Yeah. I mean, you only get to say it once a year."

Hearing that, Tomomi snorted again despite herself.

Minoru and Tomomi became friends and agreed to run along the Arakawa River whenever time allowed about eighteen days ago, on December 16. But the first time Minoru had spoken with Tomomi was December 3, another two weeks earlier.

However, Tomomi's memories of that time had been erased by the section chief's ability because Tomomi was attacked by a Ruby Eye called the Biter and narrowly avoided being eaten before Minoru saved her. They couldn't let her retain the memory of seeing the Biter's grotesque face. Minoru agreed with that, of course.

But as a result, Minoru had to keep on lying to Tomomi, too, even though she'd been kind enough to be his friend.

This is just what happens when getting close to people.

The more he closed the distance between himself and another person, the more likely something terrible would happen. Rather than face that possibility, Minoru had always kept away from others...until he rescued Tomomi from the Biter.

But then, Minoru chose to become friends with Tomomi a second time after her memories were erased.

He didn't want to regret that choice. At least as far as Tomomi Minowa was concerned, he wanted to accept and overcome whatever might happen in the future.

"Huh...?"

Tomomi suddenly took a step closer to Minoru, causing him to wonder, in a panic, if she'd read his mind.

But no, her eyes were on Minoru's right hand that had slipped out from the sleeve of his Windbreaker. Reflexively, he tried to pull back, but he was already too late.

"Utsugi, what happened to your hand?! Are you hurt?!"

The girl's expression was full of concern as she came even closer, so Minoru hastily shook his head.

"N-no, it's fine, I just fell on it a bit hard. It doesn't even hurt anymore."

Minoru tried to flex the fingers of his raised right hand as he spoke. The thin plastic cast had different parts for each finger, but at a glance, it just looked like his hand was wrapped in a bandage.

"Okay..."

Tomomi gave a sigh of relief, but her brow was still furrowed.

"Honestly, Utsugi. You're an athlete, too, so you have to take care of your body!"

"I—I don't know if I'm really an athlete..."

"If you weren't, you wouldn't be out running right at the beginning of the new year!"

Tomomi finally smiled again after saying that, but then her face became suspicious again. Minoru worried that she'd found a new injury, but this time, she'd discovered something else: the drinking valve peeking through Minoru's collar.

"Are you wearing a hydro, Utsugi?"

Assuming that she was referring to a hydration pack, Minoru nodded.

"Y-yeah. I get thirsty easily, even in winter."

"I totally get that. I want to bring water along sometimes, too, but I never end up doing it... Hey, can I have a little of yours?"

Minoru was taken aback by Tomomi's innocent grin.

"Wha—?! B-but..."

He wanted to say that he'd just had his mouth on the valve earlier, but realizing that would be a childish response, he quickly came up with something else.

"Um... Th-the pack's on my back, so the water is totally warm..."

"Ha-ha, so you do say stuff like 'totally.'"

"Huh? Oh, uh, I guess..."

"It's totally fine! Cold water's not good for your stomach anyway."

Minoru had no counter for that.

"O-okay, then... Here."

Once Minoru pulled the tube out from his collar as far as it would go, Tomomi accepted it without hesitation, bringing it to her lips and taking a drink.

Minoru's powerfully negative instincts warned him that Tomomi would probably shout "It's waaarm!" or "Grooooss!" and spit it out, but nothing of the sort happened. In fact, she gulped down a good 70 percent of the remaining three hundred milliliters left in the pack before letting out a satisfied sigh.

"Ahh, that's much better! Thank you sooo much, Utsugi."

"D-don't mention it..."

"I'm impressed, actually! Usually water in a hydro-pack ends up tasting like plastic, but that wasn't bad at all."

"R-really..."

That was because the built-in hydration pack developed by the SFD used a high-tech, tough-to-pronounce material called polyphenylene sulfide instead of regular polyethylene, but he couldn't explain that to Tomomi.

"...Apparently, if you put baking soda in there for a while before using it, the plastic smell will go away."

Tomomi's eyes widened at this knowledge, which was a bit of trivia Minoru had overheard somewhere.

"Wow, I didn't know that! I'll have to try it out when I get home!"

"I think it was about five percent..."

...Now that was yet another lie.

Of course, it was the SFD that troubled him, not the random trivia about baking soda; but in the past few weeks, Minoru had become painfully aware that lying by omission was a form of dishonesty, too.

He and Tomomi had been in the same class in the second year of junior high, but at the time, they hardly ever spoke. After that, they wound up attending the same high school and started chatting regularly after running into each other on the bank of the Arakawa River... or at least, that was what Tomomi thought.

But a major event was missing from that version of events.

If the Ruby Eye Biter hadn't attacked, Minoru and Tomomi probably wouldn't have gotten this close. Most likely, Minoru would have been seized by his usual fear of remaining in people's memories and tried to distance himself from her.

The main reason that he didn't do that was guilt over the fact that he alone knew Tomomi was missing important memories. Even he understood that it would be terrible to reject her when she asked him to be friends after forgetting so much.

But as they became better friends, the number of lies increased every time he spoke with her.

If only the government would formally announce the existence of Third Eyes—revealing the Ruby Eyes who attacked humans and the Jet Eyes who fought against them. Then he could just tell Tomomi and Norie everything, letting him ease his conscience.

But though he might think that from time to time, Minoru knew he couldn't really handle having the people around him know that he was a member of a "righteous organization that fights evil." In the end, all he could do was continue hiding for as long as possible.

As these thoughts churned in his mind, Tomomi took the valve again and drained the rest of the water.

"Ah, sorry, Utsugi! I drank it all..."

"Wha...? Oh, um, it's okay. I already had some earlier."

"Eh-heh-heh...thanks."

Tomomi handed the tube back to him, and it snapped into place as the tiny magnet on the valve connected with the metal plate built into his collar.

Glancing around, Minoru realized that it was starting to get brighter out. Tomomi squinted toward the east into the dazzling glare of the morning sun.

"Our first year of high school will be over soon…"

After her abrupt murmur, Minoru tilted his head.

"Isn't it a little early for that? We still have three months left."

"Three months'll go by in no time! I mean, I still feel like our entrance ceremony was just a few days ago!"

"Th-that's something…"

It feels like it's been ages to me, Minoru was about to say, but then he shut his mouth. Come to think of it, it did feel like the four months since the Third Eye had entered his body—especially starting from the encounter with Biter—had been so hectic that they'd passed by ten times faster.

Maybe I'll ask the Professor why our perception of time changes like that…, Minoru thought as he opened his mouth again.

"Well, should we head back so we don't waste any time, then?"

Tomomi blinked and responded in a strangely flustered tone.

"N-no, um, I didn't mean it like that…"

"Huh…? Like what?"

"Uh…n-nothing, never mind! C'mon, let's go!"

Spinning her arms in circles, Tomomi started running north on the bank without waiting for Minoru's reply.

Hurrying after her small silhouette, Minoru caught up alongside her. Glancing over at him, Tomomi raised her pace. Thirteen kilometers per hour…as the pride of the girls' track team, Tomomi was certainly able to attain speeds that Minoru might not have been able to keep up with before, but now he didn't even feel any shortness of breath.

However, looking too composed would seem unnatural, so he tried to breathe a little more heavily. Feeling a fresh wave of guilt for adding yet another layer of deception, Minoru tried to cover it by speaking to her between breaths.

"By the way…which distance is your main specialty, Minowa?"

"The three-kilometer run since we started high school."

"Wow…and what's the winning time for the inter-high championship…?"

"It's been around nine minutes recently."

"Nine minutes…which means…"

After a brief period of mental math, Minoru gave a little shout of surprise.

"Over twenty kilometers per hour?! You have to run that fast for three kilometers?!"

Tomomi laughed wryly, as if to imply that it was a little late to ask this now.

"Well, yeah. I mean, for the Olympic men's marathon, they have to run around that speed for forty-two kilometers!"

"R-really…"

Nodding absently, Minoru turned his attention toward the sphere embedded in his breastbone.

He hadn't seriously measured his time since gaining the Third Eye, but he doubted he could finish a full marathon at a speed of twenty kilometers per hour even now. So as far as raw physical abilities were concerned, the Third Eye still didn't necessarily make its host into a superhuman that exceeded normal limits.

Now that he thought about it, if Third Eye hosts all became as physically strong as Olympic gold medalists, surely the government would try to use that somehow. At the very least, they'd probably want to administer a physical fitness test. Since that wasn't happening, clearly the government also knew that Third Eye users wouldn't automatically win in a competition against true Olympic athletes.

Feeling just a little bit better, Minoru took a deep breath of the cold midwinter air.

Then, as if she were aiming for this moment of vulnerability—

From his left side, there came a completely unexpected question.

"Hey, Utsugi. Do you want to stop by my place?"

"Oh, sure… Wait, what?!"

After nodding automatically, Minoru jumped several centimeters in the air.

Once he managed to land without falling, he peered at Tomomi's face from a strange angle. Since she was looking straight ahead and breathing in an orthodox 2:2 rhythm, it was impossible to tell what she was thinking. Her cheeks and ears were a little bit red, but that was probably just because of the near-freezing air.

As Minoru struggled to respond, Tomomi spoke again without taking her eyes off the road ahead.

"Our extended family in the boonies sends us homemade mochi every year for New Year's, but we never manage to finish them. So I thought it might be nice if you could help us out a little?"

"I...see..."

Maybe it was his imagination, but she seemed to be speaking a little faster than usual. Minoru thought hard about how he could refuse.

That's right... He had no choice but to refuse. Suddenly going over to her house and eating her family's rice cakes would be way out of line. He'd probably have to meet Tomomi's family, too, and he had zero faith in his own ability to handle a situation that would undoubtedly put him into so many memories.

Besides, he was supposed to go and visit Suu Komura today. He couldn't be off enjoying himself at a friend's house...especially a girl's... while a fellow SFD member who saved his life was still fighting for her own in the ICU.

Figuring it was best to use a harmless excuse like "my family is making breakfast for me," Minoru drew a breath to speak.

Then he finally noticed how tightly Tomomi's hands were clenched as they rhythmically swung back and forth at her sides.

Tomomi Minowa wasn't the kind of person who was naturally social, either. At least in middle school, he remembered that she'd been rather isolated, whether of her own accord or because the other girls kept their distance from her.

So for Tomomi to invite a boy from a different class to her home, even if they were jogging buddies, probably took more courage than Minoru could imagine. If he refused right away, she would certainly regret inviting him in the first place. Then she would only remember this interaction as a bitter, painful disappointment.

Tomomi already had her memories of Biter erased. Minoru didn't want to cause her any more pain.

...Even if that might just be his own ego talking again.

With that in mind, Minoru took another breath, checked the watch on his wrist, and spoke.

"It's still pretty early... Won't it bother your family if you have some-one over?"

Right away, a smile brightened Tomomi's face, and she turned her head and upper body to face Minoru.

"No, it's totally fine! My whole family is made of early birds."

"Really...? Then I guess I'll take you up, if that's all right..."

"Eh-heh-heh, make sure to eat a lot!"

Minowa bumped Minoru's left shoulder playfully with her still-clenched right hand, then quickened her pace even more.

After running for a while, the two approached a silver U-shaped car barrier. The Hanekura Bridge bumper—a place where Tomomi said that *whenever I go past there, I find my feet stopping and my chest tightens.* Even with her memories erased, the fear she felt when the Biter attacked her had left its mark on her heart.

But this morning, Tomomi was able to pass right by the traffic barrier without even slowing down, as if she hadn't even noticed she was passing it. Following her past the fateful spot, Minoru hoped with all his heart that those terrifying memories would soon be gone completely from her mind.

After they crossed Hanekura Bridge and left the bank of the Arakawa River behind, the two headed north up prefectural road No. 57.

Of course, Minoru didn't know where Tomomi Minowa's home was, but it presumably wasn't far away since they had been in the same middle school. As he thought about this, he followed Tomomi to a point where the road turned east, across the Kamogawa River into a residential area. Drawing a straight line from there to Minoru's house probably wouldn't even take a third of a mile.

Tomomi stopped in front of a still new, single-family house with white-tiled outer walls and smiled.

"This is my house."

"Wow... What a nice home. My house probably isn't more than a ten-minute walk from here, actually."

At his casual reply, Tomomi brought her face near his.

"Really? Where's your house, Utsugi?"

"Well, um... Along the road we were just on, Route 57, there's a tra-ditional sweets maker... Do you know where I mean? It's not far from there..."

"Whaaat? I go there all the time to buy fresh-baked castella cake!"

Tomomi came even closer with her eyes wide, so Minoru leaned his upper body away as he nodded.

"Y-yeah, those are really good...fluffy..."

"Right?!"

With a big smile, Tomomi finally stepped away. Puffing out a long breath, she held her stomach with both hands.

"Ah, geez, just thinking about it is making me hungry... C'mon, Utsugi, let's go eat that mochi!"

With that, Tomomi headed toward the entrance, but Minoru hesitated.

"Um, Minowa, are you sure it's all right for me to come over unannounced like this...?"

"I told you, it's fine!"

"But I mean... I'm probably smelly from all that running..."

"Hmm?"

Tomomi quickly came up to him again and sniffed the air.

"Nah, you're fine. But if you're that worried about it, you wanna use our shower?"

"N-no, thanks, it's not that big of a deal!"

Minoru shook his head wildly, while Tomomi giggled as she hopped onto the tiled porch. Minoru followed after her, resigned.

Ten minutes later...

How on earth did things end up like this...?

Sitting stiffly on the floor, Minoru pondered this as his fingers moved busily.

Grasped firmly in his hands was the controller of the latest gaming console. The TV in front of him displayed a soccer game. Next to him, an elementary school boy shouted enthusiastically. And curled up on his lap was a gray tabby cat.

"Raaah, Inazuma shoooots!"

The boy shrieked as one of the players on the screen attempted a middle shot. However, Minoru's goalie jumped into the ball's path and knocked it away.

"Nooo! How'd you get that?! You're good!"

"Th-thanks..."

Minoru cleared the loose ball as he responded. The screen scrolled away quickly.

Minoru wasn't very good at games and hadn't actually played this kind much at all. Since moving in with Norie, his life had little to do with video games or mobile games, and he never really went over to friends' houses to play them, either. He had a faint memory of playing on a retro game machine with his older sister Wakaba before the incident, but he didn't remember the title.

The fact that he was still able to play the current-generation soccer game with all its complicated controls was probably—no, it was most definitely—because of the Third Eye. Because of his experience fighting Ruby Eyes when every second counted, he was able to concentrate so intently that time seemed to slow down for him.

But because of the adenosine nonaphosphate that Professor Riri Isa had told him about, he couldn't just be happy that his reflexes had improved. After all, it was entirely possible that the Third Eye was synthesizing some strange chemical substance in his body that was having an effect on his brain functions.

As he thought about all this, Minoru's fingers almost moved automatically to manipulate the buttons and joysticks, guiding the athlete marked with a green cursor toward the opposing team's goal. Luckily, or maybe unluckily, his right thumb, index, and middle finger were mostly unharmed, so he had no trouble using the controller. He dribbled and passed his way through four enemy players and took a shot at the goal. Grazing the hand of the goalie as he stretched his arm out to its limits, the ball slammed firmly into the upper left corner of the goal net.

"Gaaaah, you got meeee!"

Shouting dramatically, the boy flopped backward onto the floor, controller still in his hand. Then he turned toward Minoru bitterly.

"Was that really your first time playing this game, Minoru?"

Feeling a little embarrassed at being addressed so casually by a boy he'd just met, Minoru nodded.

"Y-yeah. But I read the instructions before we started."

"Who are you supposed to be, Amuro?"

...*Who's that?*

Minoru stared at the boy blankly and was greeted with an astonished expression, but before the child could explain, someone shouted from the dining room.

"Hey! Sou! You're supposed to only call him by his last name, Utsugi!"

Minoru turned to see Tomomi, who was in the middle of preparing food, waving her chopsticks threateningly. Her bespectacled mother, who was standing by her side, immediately pulled on the sleeve of her jersey.

"Dear, don't wave the chopsticks around like that!"

"But Sou was..."

"Just bring me a serving plate from the kitchen."

"All riiight."

Sitting nearby the mother and daughter pair and reading the newspaper was Tomomi's father, who also wore glasses. Since he had come over to their house without any notice, Minoru wanted to at least help with the food; but Tomomi's younger brother Souta, a fifth grader, dragged him over to play video games, and now he was rooted in place because of the cat that had curled up on his lap.

Grinning smugly as his older sister got a scolding, Souta sat up and resumed the soccer game.

"All right, Minoru, I'm gonna get you back this time..."

Immediately, though, his mother's voice cut in.

"Sou, we're about to eat, so don't start another game!"

Minoru expected another quarrel, but Souta was surprisingly quick to yield, turning off the console with a reluctant "all riiight."

When Souta stood up, the tabby on Minoru's knees also deigned to return to the floor after a nice long stretch. Minoru stood as well, following the boy into the dining room.

The Minowa family seemed to consist of Tomomi, her younger brother, and her parents, but there were five chairs set up at the table. Noticing Minoru's presence, Tomomi gestured to the seat next to her father. "You can sit there, Utsugi."

What is Mr. Minowa going to think of his daughter's male friend suddenly showing up at their house on the third day of the national New Year's holiday...? Minoru was anxious, but he obediently sat where he was told. He felt awkward wearing his Windbreaker at the table, but all he had underneath was a tight-fitting undershirt, so he couldn't remove it.

Though he'd already done so when he first introduced himself, Minoru felt he should apologize again for intruding on the family's time together. But before he could open his mouth, Tomomi spoke instead.

"How many mochi do you want in your New Year's soup, Utsugi?"

"Oh…um…t-two, please…"

Minoru was flustered about receiving food before the family patriarch but apparently, that order had already been decided.

"Papa's having two as well! What about you, Sou?"

"Three!" Souta replied cheerfully. Tomomi nodded and returned to the kitchen. After a few minutes, she returned with a tray carrying a set of five genuine lacquerware bowls full of traditional New Year's soup.

The soup she placed in front of Minoru was just as genuine as the bowl containing it.

There were two mochi seared on the bottom, as well as grilled chicken, mustard spinach, carrots, finely sliced mushrooms, honeywort, and thin cuts of golden yuzu. Minoru did a fair amount of cooking, but he always prioritized conservation of time and effort, so he couldn't help but voice his admiration.

"Th-this looks amazing… It's three days after New Year's, but you still made such incredible New Year's soup…"

"Where I come from, we eat it every day for the first three days of the New Year."

Sitting at his right, Mr. Minowa responded in a calm voice.

"It's also customary to increase the amount of mochi by one each day."

Tomomi's father put the newspaper down on the tatami mat as he spoke, causing Minoru to gulp nervously before he continued to voice his thoughts.

"Wow…adding that many mochi to the soup from New Year's Day must make the second and third days tough."

"Ha-ha, that's exactly right. The kids get pretty sick of it when they're stuck eating five or six of them…"

Mr. Minowa gave a surprisingly cheerful laugh, and Souta, sitting at the head of the table, got caught up in the moment.

"I can eat six, no problem! Sis, I want six mochi!"

"No way, stupid. You'd never finish them!"

"I'm not stupid! And I definitely can!"

"Eat the three in front of you first!"

As he watched the brother and sister's exchange, slightly concerned that it would turn into a fight...

Suddenly, Minoru realized that tears were welling up in his eyes. It took a moment before he understood why.

The sight of Tomomi and Souta had stirred up deeply buried memories.

If he opened the lid on them now, he would undoubtedly cry. Forcing himself to think about anything else, he casually wiped the tears away with his fingertips.

Barely managing to swallow the emotions that he was feeling more and more keenly, Minoru let out a little sigh. When he looked up, he locked eyes with Tomomi, who was looking at him strangely.

Fortunately, though, before Tomomi could say anything, Mrs. Minowa returned from the kitchen. She placed large plates filled with fish paste, rolled omelets, herring roe, and so on in the center of the table, then sat down across from Mr. Minowa.

"Utsugi, be sure to eat lots of the other New Year's dishes, too. Tomomi, hurry up and sit down!"

"Okaaay."

Tomomi sat down in front of Minoru, and Mr. Minowa picked up his chopsticks.

The family of four chorused their thanks for the food in perfect unison, with Minoru joining in a step late. Then they all picked up their soup bowls.

As soon as the clear broth entered his mouth, rich flavors spread across his taste buds.

Until the incident eight years ago, the Utsugi family must have eaten New Year's soup together every year, too, but he couldn't remember the taste anymore.

Still, the flavor and warmth that washed over Minoru felt somewhat nostalgic.

After the meal, Souta insisted on challenging Minoru to a rematch, so it was around half past eight by the time he left the Minowa house.

Norie was probably awake at this point. He'd let her know via text that he'd already had breakfast, but she would definitely want to know exactly what happened. Minoru's stomach was heavy with food, but he figured he'd run home anyway.

Just as he raised his arms to stretch, he heard the door opening, and Tomomi's voice rang out behind him.

"Oh, Utsugi, wait a second!"

Turning around, he saw Tomomi jogging toward him in sandals. She held up the plastic bag in her right hand around chest height and handed it to Minoru.

"Here, eat this at home."

"Huh...?"

Peering inside, he saw two plastic containers filled to bursting with New Year's food and sliced mochi.

"O-oh, no, I couldn't possibly take all this after everything your family fed me already..."

Flustered, he tried to return it, but Tomomi hid both hands behind her back.

"It's fine, it's fine! We always make more food than we can possibly eat. Besides, I drank all the water from your hydro-pack earlier."

"Lukewarm water and homemade New Year's food definitely aren't on the same level..."

"Ah-ha-ha, in that case...you can just treat me to something next time!"

"Huh?"

As Minoru stared, dumbfounded, Tomomi grinned at him and waved. "See you on the riverbank!" And with that, she disappeared back into her house.

Reluctantly slinging the plastic bag over his right arm, Minoru bowed politely toward the Minowa residence, then headed west on the residential road.

The Yoshimizu household was a fifteen-year-old, four-bedroom single-family house that stood on the north side of the Sakura Ward of Saitama.

The precast concrete wall was a warm gray, and the roof, black. It was a fairly subdued design compared with the white outer wall and red brick of the Minowa household, but it was Norie's father Mr. Kouhei Yoshimizu, not Norie herself, who'd chosen the colors.

Mr. Yoshimizu had passed away from a brain stem hemorrhage five years ago, and Norie's mother, Tamami, had been gone long before that, so she'd been living alone with Minoru ever since. Minoru felt guilty for burdening her so much—even before the Third Eye complicated things further—when she was only thirty-one years old, but he still couldn't bring himself to imagine giving up his current life.

Getting caught up in such thoughts again, Minoru drew a key from his small waist pouch and opened the front door. Immediately, the smell of coffee tickled his nose. Norie was indeed awake.

"I'm home..."

For some reason, Minoru only mumbled as he exchanged his running shoes for slippers, and the moment he entered the living room from the hallway...

"Welcome back, Mii!"

Norie greeted him with a bright smile, standing as if she'd been waiting for him.

"Th...thanks, Norie."

Minoru couldn't help wondering what was going on behind that smile as he returned the greeting. Getting a bad premonition, he was tempted to hightail it to his room as soon as possible, but first he had to hand over the plastic bag to Norie.

"Erm...did you get my text?"

"I sure did! I didn't know that you had friends who would invite you to breakfast like that, Mii!"

If it were Minoru's fellow SFD member Yumiko Azu saying these words, the tone would have been 100 percent sarcastic, but there wasn't a single trace of that in Norie's cheerful smile and fluffy short hair. She was probably just genuinely happy to hear that Minoru's social life was improving... But just as Minoru thought this, Norie's smile became a little bit mischievous.

"...So was this 'friend' the girl from before? Miss Komura?"

"Wha—?!" His voice cracked as he quickly shook his head. "N-no, it wasn't her! I-it's just a friend from school."

As he responded, a tight pain gripped his chest. Norie didn't know that Suu was seriously injured, and he couldn't tell her. He'd even had to make up a story about injuring his right hand from a fall while running.

Norie blinked for a moment, then inched closer. A sweet fragrance wafted from her petite frame, clad only in pajamas and a down jacket.

"Uh-huh... So is this friend a boy? A girl?"

"It's..."

Reflexively, Minoru wanted to shout, *A boy!* but the words caught in his throat. He was already lying to Norie about so many things. He didn't want to add even more dishonesty on top of that.

"...A girl...," he mumbled. "Her name's Minowa. She's in the track-and-field club at Yoshiki..."

Her face still close to Minoru's, Norie tilted her head thoughtfully, as if she was searching her memories.

"Huh...Miss Minowa? Wasn't she your classmate in junior high school?"

"I-I'm surprised you remember... I'd forgotten myself, to be honest..."

"Well, her name was in the school news pretty often back then. She went to all sorts of tournaments, didn't she?"

"Yeah, she's really fast. We've been running together on the Arakawa riverbank lately, and her form's so perfect that it's hard not to stare sometimes..."

As soon as he said that, he noticed that Norie's face was slipping back into a sly grin, so he quickly cleared his throat.

"A-anyway, her family ended up giving me some mochi and stuff to take home, so..."

Minoru handed the plastic bag over to Norie, who gave a little "oh my!" as she accepted it with both hands and carried it to the nearby dining table. Taking out the two plastic containers, she let slip another "oh!"

"Wow, just look at all these lovely New Year's dishes...! The mochi look delicious, too..."

She looked up, her expression a little worried.

"...What do you want to do? Should we...celebrate New Year's?"

"......"

Minoru didn't answer right away, instead turning his head downward slightly.

The Yoshimizu household generally didn't celebrate holidays. This extended not only to Valentine's Day and Christmas but even their birthdays as well as New Year's Eve and Day. The only exceptions were the visits to the graves of Minoru's family members and Norie's parents on the anniversaries of their deaths.

The reason for this was that when Minoru first came to the house, he'd ended up crying on days like Christmas and birthdays because they reminded him of his sister and parents. After some discussion, Norie and Mr. Yoshimizu had decided not to celebrate any yearly occasions until Minoru was able to handle it without needing to shed tears. Even so, he still received presents and such, so all that had really happened was that Norie and Mr. Yoshimizu had lost the chance to celebrate events that should've been happy memories.

Of course, now that he was sixteen, Minoru didn't cry so easily, even if he remembered his family's faces. Nonetheless, he had never been able to speak up and suggest that they start celebrating holidays again.

The reason for this was probably that somewhere deep in his heart, he instinctively rejected change. Time always seemed to slow to a halt when he was at home, and he was afraid of what would happen if it started to move again.

But sooner or later, he had to accept that some changes were inevitable. In reality, Minoru's daily life had already been drastically altered by the Third Eye. Among those changes, there were some that he had even chosen himself. So he couldn't try to make Norie alone stay the same forever.

"......Yeah."

Minoru looked up and nodded firmly.

"Let's do it. Celebrate New Year's. I'll go buy the ingredients to make the soup."

This time it was Norie's turn to gaze silently at Minoru for a moment, but finally she broke into a kind smile.

"Okay, Mii..."

Adjusting her posture, she bowed formally.

"Happy New Year. Let's have another good year together!"

2

The fastest route from Minoru's house in Saitama's Sakura district to SFD Headquarters in the Toyama 3-chome area of Shinjuku was to take the JR Saikyou line from the nearby Yonohonmachi Station to Ikebukuro, then transfer to the Tokyo Metro Fukutoshin line and get off at Nishiwaseda. It took about an hour and a half from door-to-door.

If Yumiko came to pick him up on her beloved Mach 0.7 bike, that time dropped to as little as a half hour, but he could hardly ask her to do that for reasons outside of their SFD duties. Especially when that reason was to visit Suu Komura.

That's why when Minoru left home at 10:30 a.m., he didn't reach SFD Headquarters in Toyama Park until noon exactly.

Taking the antique elevator to the fifth floor and trying to ignore the slightly unnerving sound it made, Minoru walked through the door as it opened.

"Excuse me."

He automatically uttered the phrase that had become his accustomed greeting and entered the large room that made up the entire fifth floor. But as soon as he'd taken a few steps inside, a strange feeling of discomfort stopped him in his tracks.

He realized the reason for this almost immediately.

It was quiet. There was no trace of the usual background noise of Olivier Saito's games being played on the big-screen TV in the center of the room, the sounds of DD cooking up some creative cuisine in the kitchen, or even the usual irritated greeting from Yumiko Azu that she would give along with a short wave from her sprawled-out position on the couch. The watery white sunlight of winter filtered into a room that was wrapped in complete silence.

...*But the Professor should be here, at least*...

Swapping his sneakers for slippers, Minoru placed his messenger bag on the sofa that Yumiko normally occupied before heading for the west side of the enormous room, instinctively keeping his footsteps quiet.

The SFD's field supervisor, known as "the Speculator," Professor Riri Isa had a dedicated lab in one corner of the room, separated by a white partition. Walking around the dividing screen, Minoru gazed around at the space full of countless shelves, experiment tables, and mysterious equipment, but this place appeared to be empty, too…

…No, it wasn't.

In the back of the lab, poking out from the side of a mesh chair facing the window, there was a single braid tied off with a red ribbon.

Tiptoeing closer, Minoru peered into the chair only to find a cherubic young girl fast asleep in the sunshine.

With her braided hair, printed hoodie, and culotte skirt, she was the spitting image of an elementary school student, but the white lab coat she wore and the wireless keyboard in her lap disrupted that childlike image. Her complexion didn't look terribly healthy, either. She'd probably been up all night working on something.

It was almost the appointed time now, but he didn't want to wake a young child from her nap, so he tried to back away quietly.

However, before he'd gone even one meter, the girl seemed to faintly detect his presence, and her eyes snapped open.

After blinking a few times, her large brown eyes focused on Minoru. A faint smile appeared on her lips, then curved down into a disapproving expression.

"…Mikkun, it isn't very proper to sneak a look at a lady's sleeping face."

Her rebuke sounded like it was coming from someone much older, bringing Minoru to automatically duck his head in a flustered apology.

"S-sorry, Professor… I mean, no, that's not what I was doing! You seemed tired, so I thought I'd just wait over there…"

"Hmm… Ah, is it that late already? I suppose I should be the one to apologize, then… The sunlight felt so good that I just dozed right off."

Professor Riri looked out the window as she spoke, so Minoru followed her gaze.

The window of the housing complex's fifth floor provided a clear view over the tall trees of Toyama Park. Since it was the middle of winter, most of the trees were bare, but the sight of the pale sun over the frigid atmosphere was so tranquil that it could certainly lull any onlooker to sleep.

"…On a day like this, it'd be great to sit in a *kotatsu* eating oranges and such…"

Minoru mumbled this without thinking, and the Professor crossed her arms and made a thoughtful "hmm."

"*Kotatsu*... A low, heated table, eh? True enough, SFD Headquarters has no such equipment set up at present..."

Glancing at the clock on the wall, she nodded with a serious expression.

"The hospital appointment is at two o'clock. Since it's only you and I leaving here, I thought we could have a short meeting until then, but... before that, Mikkun, could you help me for a moment?"

"Y-yes, of course, but...?"

"What? It's nothing major. Just a little bit of heavy lifting... I believe it should be in Mr. Lindenberger's room."

There's that mysterious German name again...at least, I think it's German. I don't actually know for sure.

It had come up periodically throughout Minoru's time with the SFD, so it seemed to be the name of another member, but Minoru had yet to meet him.

As Minoru dealt with a sudden wave of anxiety, the Professor spun her chair around halfway to face the PC monitor on the desk and flicked the mouse around for a moment. Then she looked up and nodded again.

"According to the equipment list, it is indeed still stored in the walk-in closet in room 303. Sorry, but would you mind getting it for me? I'll text the room's occupant to let him know you're coming."

"...Just to be clear, what am I picking up exactly?"

The elementary school–aged commander gave Minoru a satisfied grin.

"A *kotatsu* set, of course."

Crossing back through the still-empty room, Minoru took the elevator to the third floor, entering the shared corridor there.

He'd been to the fourth floor before, where Yumiko and her former partner Sanae Ikoma lived, but this was his first time setting foot on the third. Like the fourth floor, the four rooms of this area were presumably the private rooms of other SFD members, but Minoru didn't know who lived where.

For the time being, he proceeded to the door of room 303 as instructed by the Professor.

Yumiko's front door had a handwritten nameplate that read "Azu Ikoma," but this room's nameplate was still blank. Apparently, though, this was where the SFD member named Lindenberger lived.

Mentally picturing an older German gentleman with a mustache,

Minoru timidly pressed the doorbell. An old-fashioned electronic *ding-dong* sound echoed inside the room.

Five seconds…ten seconds…twenty seconds passed, and still no response. Minoru pressed the button again, but the result was the same.

"……Hmm…"

After hesitating for a short while, Minoru placed his hand on the doorknob. He expected to find the door locked and return to the fifth floor, but instead the old-fashioned rotary knob turned without resistance, and the door cracked open.

Double-checking that this was indeed room 303, Minoru pulled the door open. Immediately, he was greeted by a strong whiff of dust, causing him to grimace instinctively.

Covering his nose and mouth with his right hand, Minoru peered around inside, but like the hallway, the living room was almost completely dark. Apparently, the curtains and even the storm shutters were closed.

"Um… Hello?"

Minoru poked his head in through the doorway, but there was still no response. Was the tenant sleeping or just not at home? Either way, he couldn't just barge in uninvited.

Thinking to call the Professor to seek her directions, Minoru started taking his smartphone out of his pocket. But before he completed this action, he noticed a tiny glint of light in the corner of his eye.

"……?"

Furrowing his eyebrows, Minoru squinted and found that the source of the light was a thin thread strung up between the hallway and the floor.

It was a spiderweb. The light from the hallway was reflecting off it.

Since it was midwinter now, the spider that made the web was no longer there, and the web itself was falling apart. In other words, it was a considerably old web, and since it was stretched across the entryway, nobody had come into or out of this room for several months.

"…What, so it's just a vacant room…?"

Mumbling to himself, Minoru put his phone back in the inner pocket of his mountain parka. The Professor must have gotten the room number wrong. In which case, there was a good chance that the table he was here to pick up wasn't in this room, but he wouldn't know unless he took a look.

Searching around the entrance again, he noticed that there wasn't a single pair of shoes on the tiled floor. Thinking that he should have noticed something was off sooner, he opened the shoe cupboard. It was mostly empty, aside from two pairs of cheap vinyl slippers and a single shoehorn.

First, he took out the shoehorn and used it to remove the spiderweb blocking the entrance. Then, he took out one of the dusty pairs of slippers into the hallway, changing out of his sneakers.

"...Okay, I'm coming in."

Minoru announced his intent in a small voice, despite the fact that the room was clearly vacant, before stepping into the inner corridor. Locating a light switch by feeling around, he flipped it on, and an LED light bulb lit up faintly.

The structure of the room was probably the same as Yumiko's, so the walk-in closet the Professor mentioned was probably through the closed door on the right of the corridor. In Yumiko's place, she had informed him that he would be thrown off the balcony if he opened hers. With that thought in mind, he carefully opened the door in question to find a Western-style room about thirty meters around. He tried turning on the lights as before, but the metal rosettes installed on the ceiling were bare, so nothing happened when he flipped the switch.

If he opened the windows and storm shutters, there would probably be plenty of sunlight; but that seemed like a hassle, so instead he took out his smartphone again and put it in flashlight mode. This smartphone, which the SFD had provided him with, was apparently another piece of specially made equipment, so the battery wouldn't decrease much even with heavy use.

Illuminated by Minoru's phone light, the room was as empty as expected. There wasn't a single piece of furniture, but he saw his objective on the southern wall—a closet with a folding door. Breathing a sigh of relief as he approached, he pulled it open with one hand.

The walk-in closet was apparently being used as a storeroom, as it was full of stacks of cardboard boxes instead of clothes. Most of them were nonperishable foods, like mineral water, canned goods, and cupped ramen, but what he was looking for was in the far right corner: a large cardboard box with the word *kotatsu* on the side.

Minoru moved to drag it out, but then something else caught his eye. Right next to the *kotatsu* was a cardboard box marked with an energy bar logo, the seal open and the lid slightly ajar. Peeking inside, he saw that the contents of the twenty-four cases inside were about halfway gone.

Most likely, someone knew these goods were here and snuck away energy bars on the sly. It could be Olivier, Yumiko, or maybe even the Professor herself... *So maybe I should help myself to a box, too?* Minoru thought for an instant, but of course he did nothing of the kind, pulling out only the *kotatsu* box he originally came for.

Closing the door of the closet and putting his smartphone away, Minoru lifted the box with both hands. It was surprisingly heavy but certainly nothing his Third Eye–strengthened body couldn't handle.

Minoru thought about the mystical substance of adenosine nonaphosphate being used up in the muscle cells of his arms as he carried the box into the hallway, then went back inside to put away the slippers and shoehorn and turn off the LED bulb.

"...Sorry for intruding," he mumbled as he left, but of course there was no answer.

Once he closed the door and lifted the *kotatsu* box again, Minoru headed to the elevator.

The Professor had said she just needed "a bit of heavy lifting," but Minoru's task didn't end there, as he next had to assemble the *kotatsu* from the box. After installing the four legs on the body, situating it on the rug in front of the TV, covering the bottom with the accompanying blanket, and placing the board on top, Minoru paused to catch his breath. Then he plugged it into the power strip, flipped the switch, made sure the inside glowed red before looking over to the west side of the room.

"Um, Professor, the *kotatsu*'s all put together..."

But before he could finish speaking, the girl in the lab coat came rushing out of her booth and dove into the *kotatsu* with cartoonish zeal.

Minoru looked on speechlessly as the Professor's face shifted from expressionless to ridiculously relaxed in a matter of seconds.

"...Mm-hmm, I knew it, nothing beats this. It feels like so long since I've remembered that such a wondrous heating device exists in Japan..."

"That's, uh…"

…*a bit of an overstatement*, Minoru wanted to say, but he managed to keep his mouth shut.

Professor Riri Isa had made contact with the Third Eye four months ago and gained the speculation ability—or rather, had it planted within her. Since then, she had rarely returned home, opting to shut herself up in SFD Headquarters.

Minoru had assumed the "rarely" part until today. Even though she was their commander, she was still a ten-year-old girl in her fourth year of elementary school, so he figured she probably went home on the weekends.

However, since she was here in spite of the New Year's three-day holiday, that must have meant she never went home at all.

Apparently, Yumiko and Olivier had told their parents that they were staying at a school dormitory. They really did go to school from here, though, and occasionally went home to their families.

But the Professor…it seemed bizarre that a ten-year-old girl could stay out for so long without her family members being alarmed. She couldn't exactly get away with claiming to have transferred to a boarding school. Then what exactly did the SFD—Chief Himi—do…?

On the verge of voicing his questions aloud, Minoru instead abandoned that line of thought. Since he was refusing to move into headquarters himself, it didn't seem right for him to pry into her business.

Almost as if she knew what Minoru was thinking, Professor Riri looked up at him and smiled with an innocence befitting her age.

"Thanks for going to all that trouble, Mikkun. Don't just stand there—why don't you come under here, too? We don't have any mandarin oranges, though, sorry."

"Ahh… Should I check in the fridge?"

"No, I was going through it last night, so I'm unfortunately quite certain about that. And since DD's back home with his family right now, we don't have any other food, either."

"Oh, I see…"

At first, Minoru thought maybe he should have swiped some energy bars from room 303 after all, but then he finally remembered what was in his own bag.

"Oh, that's right! Please wait a moment."

"Hmm…?"

The Professor gave him a dubious look as he retrieved his messenger bag from the nearby sofa and brought it into the kitchen. There, he removed three small containers from the bag, placed the contents onto a few serving dishes, and arranged the dishes on a tray along with two plates and two sets of chopsticks. While he was at it, he brewed enough roasted green tea for two, then hurried back to the heated table.

Seeing the dishes lined up on the board, the Professor's eyes sparkled.

"What's this?! You brought mochi?!"

"I did. These ones are soy flour, these are wrapped in seaweed, and these have cheese."

"Ooh... It feels like so long since I've remembered that such a wondrous food exists in Japan..."

Repeating the same strange phrasing from before, the Professor accepted her plate and chopsticks from Minoru.

"We actually received some mochi for the first time in a long while, but my sister and I got sort of excited and ended up making way too much ourselves..."

"Hoh-hoh, you getting excited about mochi? Now that I'd like to see... So is it all right if I have a few?"

"Of course, please help yourself."

As soon as Minoru gave the go-ahead, the Professor immediately grabbed a cheese mochi with her chopsticks and popped it straight into her mouth. After she munched on it and gulped, her eyes widened with glee.

"Yum!"

"G-glad you like it. That one has homemade pizza sauce on it, too."

"Ooh, the flavor of the tomato complements it perfectly. Next is the seaweed-wrapped kind... Mm-hmm, now that's a very traditional flavor. This one's tasty, too!"

"Apparently, the trick is to use good soy sauce and get a little char on it."

As he conveyed the knowledge Norie had shared with him, Minoru helped himself to a piece of mochi as well. He'd just eaten the same thing a few hours ago, but it seemed to taste a little different when enjoyed under a *kotatsu*, even if it wasn't at home.

Once she'd sampled each of the flavors, the Professor took a long gulp of tea and let out a satisfied sigh.

Then, a few seconds later, she said something totally unexpected.

"...So it doesn't seem like you blame me, Mikkun."

"Huh…? B-blame you…?"

"Well, yes. For what happened…"

She lowered her head, her braids bobbing as she spoke in a quiet voice.

"…Back in Minami-Aoyama, when you, Yukko, and Oli-V battled against Liquidizer and Trancer… I didn't send in a backup unit, even though I knew it might be a difficult fight. I prioritized obtaining information about the Syndicate over your safety. Because of that, now Oli-V's in the hospital with serious injuries, and since Hinako's treatment for her severe condition didn't happen immediately, she's still in the ICU… Mikkun, you have every right to blame me."

Even after the Professor finished speaking, Minoru kept quiet for a moment.

Then he put his chopsticks down on his plate and shook his head gently.

"No… I don't have any such right to blame you, and I don't want to, either. If anything, I'm sorry for getting so emotional during our communication that day… I'm sure it was hardest on you, since you were commanding us…"

Minoru looked down, and this time the Professor was silent for a moment.

He heard the sound of cloth rustling, followed by small footsteps. At first, he thought she was leaving, but instead the Professor walked around the *kotatsu*, sat down beside Minoru's left, and stuck her skinny legs back under the blanket.

"Er, um…"

As Minoru sat stiffly, unsure of what to do, he felt a small weight against his side. Professor Riri was leaning against him. Eventually, she spoke in a faint whisper.

"…To be honest, I spent all morning preparing myself for you to be angry at me."

"Huh…?"

"My speculation ability can't read people's minds. All I could do was imagine how angry and disappointed you must be in me… But after the stuff you just said, I have no idea what I'm supposed to do."

So why are you sitting next to me, then? Minoru thought, but he didn't say it out loud. Instead, he spread out the quilt, which had gotten shoved under the table, and wrapped it around the Professor.

"...Eat more mochi, please."

Minoru moved her plate toward her, and the Professor gave a child-like nod and an "uh-huh," then picked up her chopsticks again.

In the end, the Professor ate five mochi, and Minoru ate three; he put the leftovers back into their containers and stowed them in the refrigerator, and then they returned to the lab together.

It was now one o'clock in the afternoon. Considering how long it would take to get to the hospital, they only had another twenty minutes or so, but nonetheless the Professor pulled up another mesh chair to her desk and had Minoru sit there.

"...I feel bad showing this to you before we go visit Hinako, but I wanted to share this information with you..."

With that, the Professor moved the mouse. A video played back on the seventy-plus-centimeter 8K monitor in full screen. A grating engine noise emitted from the speakers.

"...What's this...?"

"It's a video from the body camera of a Special Task Squad member infiltrating the Syndicate base, which we located with the information you got for us on New Year's."

"......!! The...the STS?"

The Professor nodded silently at a breathless Minoru.

The official name of the STS was the Japan Self-Defense Forces Ground Staff Office Operational Support Intelligence Department, Special Task Squad. It was practically impossible to figure out what the organization did from its name, which was even longer than the SFD's, but apparently, it was a unit of Jet Eye holders within the Self-Defense Forces.

The video on the monitor showed soldiers dressed all in black, sitting side by side. The lighting was low, so they almost appeared to be nothing but silhouettes, but Minoru could tell they were soldiers from the large automatic rifles each of them carried. Judging by the shaking on-screen and the noise, he thought they were likely inside a helicopter.

Gulping as he watched intently, Minoru heard a man's low voice beneath the engine sound.

"Sixty seconds to the target. Prepare for fast rope descent."

The camera moved, capturing a full view of the inside of the helicopter. There seemed to be six soldiers, including the one filming.

"A-are all of them Jet Eyes…?" Minoru whispered, but the Professor quickly shook her head.

"No, none of them. They're all ordinary humans…though they are highly trained, elite soldiers."

"Huh? But isn't the STS a group of Jet Eyes…?"

"I'll explain afterward. For now, just watch closely."

With that, Minoru had no choice but to swallow his questions for now.

"Thirty seconds."

When the man spoke again, the soldiers began to move. Standing up from the simple seats, they lined up with three people in front of each of the doors on the left and right of the cabin. Before long, the sound of the engine changed, and the shaking abated a little.

"Open the doors. Begin descent."

In response to the commander's hushed order, the large sliding doors were pulled back at once. Instead of city lights, all that was visible beneath the dark-violet sky was the black surface of the ocean.

The time stamp displayed in the lower right corner of the video read "12-31-2019 17:14." Minoru and the others had fought with Liquidizer and Trancer on the abandoned factory site around four p.m. that day, so this took place a mere hour later.

On the screen, the soldiers descended one after another without a lifeline, using only the two ropes hanging from the helicopter's side doors. The person recording was last to go, grabbing the ropes and jumping without hesitation. Now the scene below the hovering aircraft was finally visible—but instead of water, there were several flat rectangular buildings below. The place appeared to be some kind of reclaimed warehouse district.

"Professor… Where is this?"

The Professor gave a short reply.

"It's Keihinjima, in Ota Ward."

"Keihinjima…? Wait…"

Lately, Minoru had been spending much of his free time looking at a map of Tokyo on his smartphone so that he'd be more familiar with the lay of the land for his work as an SFD member, but it took him a little while to remember this area. If he recalled correctly, it was a small artificial island south of Ooi Pier. Which meant, in other words…

"…Isn't that just north of Haneda Airport?!"

What he meant was that he was surprised they were able to fly a heli-copter so close, but the Professor seemed to take his words in a different way and nodded with a grimace.

"That's right. The higher-ups were beside themselves when they found out the Syndicate had a base there...especially since airports are such a prime target for terrorist attacks. Instead of the small-scale reconnais-sance missions that were planned beforehand, they decided to go with an all-out armed assault."

"...But they still used regular humans instead of Jet Eyes...? If there are Ruby Eyes there, the squad will probably be wiped out in an instant by their abilities...," Minoru murmured, forgetting that this image was from three days earlier.

On the screen, the six soldiers—no, since they were Self-Defense Forces members, maybe they should be called "agents"—descended onto the site of a two-story warehouse and ran directly toward the front door. If there were any Ruby Eyes inside, surely they would notice the sound of the helicopter above, so there probably was no point in trying to hide their presence.

At the same time, though, this would have made them easy targets for the Ruby Eyes. If there were any enemies with similar powers to, say, the Igniter, they could swipe oxygen away from the whole group in a moment, and the agents would all collapse before they could do a thing.

But all this was nothing more than Minoru's speculation on events that had already occurred.

"Huh...? They're dressed sort of strangely..."

Mumbling to himself, Minoru brought his face closer to the monitor.

Unlike the STS members he'd met a few days earlier, Nishikida and Kakinari, these black-clad agents were wearing what looked like form-fitting bodysuits instead of combat uniforms. They seemed to have inner armor and power sources built into various places, but the silhouettes were sleek, and instead of the usual helmets of the Self-Defense Forces, they were wearing masks that covered their faces and entire heads.

"...Are these people really Self-Defense Forces personnel?"

This time, the Professor responded quickly to Minoru's latest question.

"They're wearing special anti–Third Eye suits, developed by the Defense Equipment Agency...that is, a joint venture between the for-mer Acquisition, Technology & Logistics Agency and the Itsuki Heavy

Industry Co. They're bulletproof, stab/slash-proof, gas-proof, heat resistant, and shock resistant... Apparently, even a 5.56 mm NATO round fired from three meters away won't penetrate them. Just about the only thing they can't ward off is radiation."

"Ah... Okay..."

Since he didn't have a lot of military knowledge, Minoru didn't really understand the details, but he could tell from the cascading list the Professor had recited that the uniforms were quite impressive.

"Incidentally, they currently cost three hundred million yen apiece."

"Th-three hundred...?"

Minoru stared aghast at the screen, where one of the agents was cutting the padlock on the sliding doors with a tool. In just a few seconds, the lock fell to the ground, and the agent opened the door by about five centimeters. Then the agent pulled out a thin cable, like the one used for Minoru's hydration pack, from the collar of the suit and pushed it into the opening. It was not a water supply valve but a camera; after a short while, the agent looked back and nodded.

Apparently, the person wearing the body camera was the commander; gesturing back, he instructed the other five members in a calm, even voice.

"We're going in."

The closest agent pulled the door wide open, and the group rushed in, readying their rifles. The commander stepped into the building last and quickly moved his flashlight-equipped rifle all across the room before declaring "clear." Apparently, the only voice being recorded was that of the person wearing the camera, the commander.

The first floor of the warehouse contained countless rows of large steel racks, but most of them were empty, with just a few cardboard boxes loaded onto the ones in the rear. The floor, which was painted green, was faintly coated in dust, giving the impression that nobody had come in or out in some time.

"Um, is this really..."

...*the Syndicate's base?* Minoru stopped short before he finished voicing his question. The size and purpose of the room seemed quite different, but its eerie emptiness did remind Minoru of the interior of the building he and Suu had broken into in Minami-Aoyama. It had the same sense of a temporary residence—a place that wouldn't be used for long.

·Just then, the five agents on the screen all pointed the barrels of their rifles at the ceiling.

"Apparently, their body heat thermosensors detected something here."

"Thermosensors...? Through the ceiling, you mean?"

"I mean, they do cost three hundred million yen... Make sure you don't miss this next part."

At the Professor's whisper, Minoru stared intently at the monitor as if trying to bore a hole through it.

The stairs to the second floor were in the back of the warehouse. The black-clad soldiers moved swiftly between the steel racks, with movements so smooth and controlled that even a novice like Minoru could tell how practiced they were.

In truth, it did seem like a gun was more powerful than almost any Third Eye holder's abilities. In which case, if those suits were as strong as the Professor said, maybe these six agents armed with assault rifles really could neutralize a Ruby Eye. Since they were gas-proof, that also meant they were completely airtight, presumably equipped with air cylinders, meaning they would've been able to withstand something like Igniter's oxygen deprivation.

Of course, if Liquidizer got a hold of them with her ability to liquefy any substance, they would still melt immediately—but even Liquidizer surely couldn't get close enough to touch them while fending off rifle bullets from every direction.

The Syndicate Ruby Eyes lurking on the second floor are probably going to be shot to pieces.

With that in mind, Minoru had to struggle to keep his eyes from straying instinctively from the video feed.

On the screen, the agents arrived in the back of the warehouse and formed a line to ascend the iron staircase. Despite how heavy the suits and rifles must have been, their footsteps were scarcely audible.

Then just as the first in line had gotten about halfway up the long staircase—

The three men in the front of the party collapsed at the knee at nearly the exact same time.

The brawny men in their high-tech suits went tumbling down the stairs, their dropped rifles following behind. The other three, including the commander, tried to catch them and stop their fall.

But at that moment, the commander emitted a low groan.

The body camera pointed up at the ceiling, then started spinning around and around. The person wearing it had begun falling down the stairs, too.

The commander reached the first floor and rolled to a halt, his remaining comrades close behind. The screen shook violently for a moment, then stopped moving altogether, still facing sideways. Three seconds later, the video ended.

Even after the window went black, Minoru kept staring for a while.

Then, turning his stiff neck slowly to his right, he looked at the Professor.

"…What…? What happened to them…?"

"Well, we know this much. All six members of the attack force were killed instantly, at just about the same time."

"Wh-why…? How could that…?"

"Why did it happen…? That I can't answer. But not because it's classified or anything. Neither I, the STS, nor even the 3E Committee that supervises both our groups have any idea what killed these men."

Minoru stared, dumbfounded, at the Professor, who was fiddling with her braid glumly.

Just a few dozen seconds ago, Minoru had been thinking this team could defeat any Ruby Eye—that maybe he and the other SFD members wouldn't have to fight anymore. But then all of them were killed in an instant, by a still-unknown cause… He couldn't wrap his head around it.

"…B-but since they died, there must be a reason…a cause of death, right?"

The Professor nodded, her right hand still clutching her braid.

"Well, yes. Of course, a detailed autopsy is being performed even as we speak. However, as soon as communication was lost with all six members, their suit monitors detected that their hearts and breathing had stopped, and the built-in AEDs couldn't revive them, so the helicopter on standby above…swept the second floor of the warehouse with heavy weapons fire. They were using M2 machine guns, so the rounds went through the floor, and all sorts of steel frames and things fell on top of the six agents. This damaged both the suits and their bodies, making it all the more difficult to identify the cause of death… Do you want me to pull up the video of the machine-gun fire?"

"No..."

Minoru refused instinctively but then considered that he shouldn't let any information go to waste and nodded instead.

"...Yes, please."

"Okay."

The Professor nodded, letting go of her braid to move the mouse with her right hand. A new window opened, and the small speakers emitted the heavy sound of an engine.

This camera seemed to be a large one fixed to the airframe of the helicopter, with a much clearer image compared with the body camera from before. The screen displayed a gray warehouse in the dark of twilight. There were no windows on the second floor, so the inside of the building couldn't be seen.

A powerful searchlight shone on the roof of the warehouse.

Then there were continuous bursts of yellow lights from the right side of the screen, and a metallic roaring sound drowned out the engine. More bullets, possibly tracer rounds, flew with a streak of red light one by one, filling the ceiling of the warehouse with holes.

In a matter of seconds, the roof collapsed from the center, exposing the interior.

The second floor of the warehouse seemed to be divided into several rooms. One room contained stacks of cardboard boxes, another had a line of clerical desks, and one even had a bed, but the machine guns mowed everything down mercilessly.

He knew this video had probably been thoroughly scrutinized already, but Minoru searched for signs of people nonetheless. However, he didn't see anyone running away, much less facing off against the armed helicopter. All four rooms were completely destroyed in less than a minute and finally collapsed along with the floor itself. Then the guns finally went silent, and Minoru started breathing again, only then realizing he had been holding his breath at all.

"......That was..."

Minoru's lips trembled as he searched for the words, continuing in a faint voice.

"That was basically all-out war, wasn't it...? Did they really do this in Japan...right in a suburb of Tokyo...?"

"They did. But this incident hasn't been reported on at all, even though it was three days ago. This strategy was clearly a huge departure from the conservative stance favored so far, though the higher-ups say it's because a Ruby Eye base so close to Haneda Airport was a highly critical situation. It's possible that there was a change in the 3E Committee or maybe even higher than that..."

The Professor's words were hard for Minoru to follow, since he didn't even know all the members of his own group, the SFD. Returning his attention to the screen, he saw that the video was still playing back, showing the searchlight trawling over the wreckage of the warehouse. Presumably, they were searching for the corpses of the Ruby Eyes who must have been on the second floor, but the light illuminated nothing but rubble.

Before Minoru could ask another question, the Professor spoke up.

"After this, they performed a thorough search along with recovering the bodies from the time of the assault, but no Ruby Eyes were found, living or dead. Besides, if a Ruby Eye *had* died, the exodus phenomenon should've occurred..."

"......So in other words, the Ruby Eye who killed those six STS members must have survived that sweep somehow and escaped...right?"

"And completely unharmed, at that. They didn't find a single drop of blood, never mind any human remains. If you ask me, a Third Eye holder who can survive a direct hit from 12.7 mm rounds would have to have an ability on par with yours, Mikkun..."

"...E-even I'm not so sure I could've survived something like that..."

"Oh, don't say that, please. Mikkun, your barrier ability is the star of hope for me and the SFD...or the shell of hope, I guess."

Minoru shrank down automatically in his seat at the strange compliment.

Of course, Minoru's shell had yet to be pierced or broken by any attack. Not Biter's jaws, which could snap through iron pipes like candy bars; not Igniter's hydrogen explosions, which had blown apart the roof of an indoor pool; not even Liquidizer's hand, which could melt steel pillars, could penetrate Minoru's shell. The SFD wasn't even sure if his ability had a physical form or not.

However, it still wasn't an all-powerful shield. He knew firsthand that it couldn't move if he was surrounded by concrete, and Minoru had smashed his right hand in order to escape, while Suu Komura sustained serious wounds in the process.

"…So this is the result of the information that Suu put her life on the line to deliver…?"

The Professor was quick to respond to Minoru's absentminded murmur.

"The data you two brought back from the safe house in Minami-Aoyama is still being analyzed. That warehouse is just the first hideout that we discovered. A PC was recovered from the rubble of that building, so we'll undoubtedly gain more information from that, too. Hinako's actions didn't go to waste."

The Professor's voice was strained with suppressed emotion.

Minoru chewed his lip as he stared at his cast-wrapped right hand, and the Professor clapped him lightly on the back.

"Well, that's all the information I have for you right now. Let's go see how Hinako's doing, shall we?"

The Professor moved to stand up, but Minoru put a hand on her right arm.

"Um, before we do that…"

"Hmm…?"

"Could you tell me…the names of the six STS agents who died?"

"……"

This time, the Professor gazed at Minoru's face silently. Then she nodded a little and recited them without looking at anything.

"All right. The commander was First Lieutenant Naohisa Nakaoka, and the team members were Sergeant Major Saburou Yarai, Sergeant Major Kakeru Tomita, Sergeant First Class Soutarou Omi, Sergeant First Class Yukimasa Nojima, and Sergeant Shinya Maki. They were all from the Ranger Corps or the Special Task Squad."

Repeating the names of the six people in his mind, Minoru closed his eyes. Jet Eyes or not, these were his comrades who were killed in the line of duty, fighting for the common goal of stopping the Ruby Eyes' murderous actions. He could never forget that sacrifice.

"…Thank you."

Minoru lowered his head. Professor Riri Isa reached for his back again, but this time instead of hitting it, she patted him gently.

3

Minoru left SFD Headquarters with the Professor, who had changed from her white lab coat into a pink down jacket. As they walked side by side along the path that crossed Toyama Park, it occurred to him that they'd never gone anywhere together before.

Minoru was a sixteen-year-old high school student, and the Professor was a ten-year-old fourth grader. This wouldn't be an unusual age difference for a pair of siblings, but Minoru's fragile mental state made him highly doubtful that he could ever pass for a good older brother. Besides, the Professor far surpassed him in terms of mental age.

Maybe he was overthinking it, but Minoru felt as if some of the mothers passing by with their young children were eyeing him suspiciously. Just as he was becoming convinced that he would be reported as a kidnapper if they kept walking like this any longer—

The Professor suddenly grabbed his left hand.

Wha—?!

Unleashing a silent scream in his mind, Minoru's legs tangled, nearly causing him to fall. Immediately, the Professor—who still had her Jet Eye strength despite being a child—shot an arm out and caught him.

"Ah… Th-thank you…"

Minoru mumbled his thanks, and the Professor smiled dryly as she whispered a response.

"Was that reaction really necessary? I was just holding your hand."

"Y-yeah, but it was just so sudden, I was startled…"

"I just thought we'd look more like siblings this way. That would make you feel a bit better, right?"

"Well…yeah, I guess…"

Minoru had often held Norie's hand as they walked when he was in elementary school, and that had never seemed unnatural, but now it was the year 2020. Did kids these days still hold hands with their younger siblings? *I'll have to ask Minowa next time I see her…*, he thought, reflecting back on Professor Riri's actions throughout the day and puzzling over everything.

Perhaps noticing the slight tilt of his head or sensing something through their linked hands, the Professor nudged him and whispered again.

"What's wrong, Mikkun?"

"Oh, nothing... I mean, um... I was just thinking that you've been a little more, uh, friendly than usual today, Professor..."

"Mnn..."

Apparently, this was news to the Professor, as it was now her turn to tilt her head in thought. After a moment, she nodded briskly.

"I suppose you might be right. I can't very well view my own actions objectively."

Minoru hesitated a moment before he responded.

"Right... Um, is there some reason...?"

Minoru knew even less about the Professor's family circumstances than he did about the others, like Yumiko and Olivier. He had wondered while they were sitting in the *kotatsu* at SFD Headquarters what kind of explanation she'd given her family, but even the idea that she had a family at all was just an assumption on his part.

Currently, Suu and Olivier were in the hospital, but DD and Yumiko were apparently at home with their families. Wasn't the Professor lonely spending New Year's alone at headquarters, with no one else around?

It was with all that in mind that he'd asked his question, but the Professor's answer was far from what he'd expected...

"Hmm, let me see... Mikkun, the SFD doesn't have any silly rules or regulations that forbid members from dating one another, you know."

"Erm...what?"

Minoru stared down at Professor Riri, who was looking up at him with a serious face.

"So if you ever manage to work out the romantic rivalry between you, Yukko, and Hinako, you won't be reprimanded or anything... Oh, or does a 'romantic rivalry' only refer to two men fighting over a woman? What's it called when it's two women, then...?"

"Isn't it just a l—? I mean, wait, no! Th-there's nothing going on between me and Suu or Yumiko!"

"I don't think Yukko would've been crying like that over 'nothing'..."

"......Please don't ever, ever say that in front of her..."

"Of course not. In any case...I suppose it's possible that I subconsciously felt left out of your little situation, and that was the cause of my behavior today."

"H...huh...?"

What's there to feel "left out" about, and why would it lead to you being extra affectionate? Minoru was very confused.

But before he could get any kind of answer, a car horn blared briefly nearby.

Looking up, he saw that a red compact car had stopped on the side of the walkway about nine meters away from them, with its hazard lights on.

"Oh, there they are."

The Professor quickened her pace without releasing Minoru's hand, so he broadened his strides as well.

As he approached the car, an Alfa Romeo Giulietta, he heard the door unlocking. The Professor let go of his hand and opened the door on the passenger's side, adding, "You sit in the back, Mikkun," so Minoru obediently climbed into the rear area, which was surprisingly spacious for a hatchback.

His nose was greeted by a faint whiff of citrus as he entered. At the same time, a voice came from the driver's seat.

"Happy New Year, Utsugi."

"Oh yes, Happy New Year...wait, Yumiko?!"

Minoru flinched back automatically as Yumiko Azu shot him a glance from the front seat, her black hair fastened in a simple red barrette.

"There's no need to look so shocked."

"I-it's just I heard that you were home with your family..."

"I came back today. I wanted to visit Komura, too."

"I...I see. Sorry about that. Thank you for driving."

Ducking his head a little, Minoru tightened his seat belt. In the passenger's seat, the Professor was also adjusting the length of her seat belt as she spoke to Yumiko.

"We're not on a mission today, so please drive safely, Yukko."

"Understood... But still, Professor..."

Yumiko glanced to her right for a moment, then quickly shook her head and pushed the start button. "No, never mind." The engine, which was considerably more vigorous than that of the average Japanese car, roared to life as the instrument panel lit up.

It was at this point that Minoru started to wonder how Yumiko had gotten a license when she was a first-year in high school like him... again. He hadn't gotten too hung up on it when Suu Komura, a middle schooler, was driving a Daihatsu Copen before, but Yumiko was wearing her usual sailor uniform with a black blazer and red ribbon, so Minoru was worried that they might get stopped by motorcycle police or something.

However, Yumiko clearly had no such concerns as they set off smoothly in the six-speed manual Giulietta.

Cruising at an easy speed past the lines of apartment buildings, they turned left on Meiji Avenue.

Minoru opened his mouth again as the speed of the car started to rise.

"So, um…this isn't the same car as before, is it? The Delica."

The car in question was a black minivan that they'd taken to the reconnaissance mission in Minami-Aoyama.

"Well, there are only three of us today, so there was no reason to take such a big car."

"But there's also that Copen that Suu was driving that time and that Agusta you had, Yumiko… Just how many vehicles does the SFD have, exactly?"

Yumiko and the Professor locked eyes for a moment, then cleared their throats at the same time.

"Well, let's just say…as many as are necessary for our mission, Mikkun."

"Uh…right…"

"I mean, James Bond has a different vehicle in practically every scene, right? And they're always super-high-class luxury cars, whether it's Jaguars or Aston Martins."

"Uh…riiight…"

…There's still an awful lot that I don't know about the SFD, Minoru couldn't help but think.

On January 3, there were few cars in the city center as the red Giulietta smoothly headed south on Meiji Avenue, turned onto Gaien West Avenue from Yasukuni Avenue, and pulled into the parking lot of the large hospital in Hiroo, Shibuya.

The place was less than a mile away from Minami-Aoyama, where they had battled with Liquidizer and Trancer on New Year's Eve. Perhaps it was excessive to use an emergency helicopter for such a short distance, but that was also reflective of how severe Suu's condition was.

Stepping out of the car, which Yumiko had parked perfectly on her first attempt, Minoru was greeted by the faint smell of disinfectant, even in the parking lot. Professor Riri Isa proceeded toward the building with a stiff expression, and Minoru and Yumiko followed.

After taking the elevator to the fourth floor, the Professor led the way past the nurses' station and proceeded into the hallway. At the end of the hall was a sturdy stainless steel door, with a guard stationed in front of it.

As the three approached, the guard snapped off a quick salute, to which the Professor responded with a silent nod. His uniform suggested he was from a private security firm, but Minoru wondered if he was connected with the police as the man operated a security device to open the door with a heavy sound.

On the other side was a completely silent space, overflowing with white light. The clean aisle continued for about nine meters, with large horizontal windows and a pair of sliding doors along the left wall.

Stopping in front of the first window, the Professor had to stand on tiptoe a little to see inside. Yumiko walked forward, looking resolute, so Minoru followed behind her.

Through the window was a spacious private room, full of machinery.

And in the center was a single wheeled bed.

About three weeks ago, Minoru had gone to the university hospital in Saitama to visit Tomomi Minowa after she was attacked by the Ruby Eye Biter. At that time, Tomomi's room had a large window with flowers on the bedside table, but the ICU room on the other side of the glass the three looked at now was far colder and mechanical, the very air heavy with tension.

Resisting the urge to press his hands and forehead against the polished glass, Minoru squinted inside intently.

There was a blanket over the bed and a cabinet of machinery in front of it, so all Minoru could see of the patient were the tips of her shoulders. But Minoru was instinctively certain that the pure-white skin peeping out of the post-op clothing belonged to Suu Komura.

"......Can we not go in, Professor?" Yumiko asked in a quiet voice on Minoru's left. The Professor answered from his right.

"Unfortunately, this is as far as we have permission to go. Hinako's vitals are stable right now, but she did just undergo surgery to treat an acute subdural hemorrhage..."

"So…she *will* wake up, won't she?"

The Professor's response to Yumiko's question was slightly delayed.

"…I believe she will. However, since Hinako's Third Eye is fused to the lower portion of her thalamus, even specialized physicians can't predict what the effect on her brain might be. We don't even know yet how Third Eyes gain energy from our bodies or whether biochemical energy is involved…"

Minoru unconsciously moved his left hand to touch the center of his chest.

The black Third Eye inside Minoru's body was embedded in the center of his breastbone, slightly above the surface of the sternum. Even just pressing on his skin, he could feel the slight protrusion, though there was no pain or sense of a foreign substance.

The Third Eye sometimes hid itself completely inside the body, like in the cases of Yumiko, Minoru, and Suu, but other times, like with Igniter or the STS member Kakinari, nearly half of it could be exposed. Nobody yet knew why these spheres had appeared or why they had latched onto humans.

But even so…

"……If the Third Eye is a living thing…surely it doesn't want to die, either."

Yumiko and the Professor turned toward Minoru as he mumbled. Feeling their gaze on him, Minoru continued.

"I think they must have a reason for falling to earth and attaching themselves to humans…a purpose for their existence. So if its host's life is in danger, I think it would try to help…even if that's just so it can keep fighting the enemy."

"……Yes, that makes sense."

The Professor nodded, her braids swaying.

"The Third Eye synthesizes incredible things inside our body, like the substance adenosine nonaphosphate. In which case…since the brain is the greatest black box of the human body, perhaps it would try to heal it in a way that would normally be impossible for us. Hinako is going to wake up again, sooner or later… I'm sure of it."

Yumiko's expression shifted inscrutably at these words.

"You're right… Komura is the strongest Jet Eye in the SFD, so she's not going to die from a little bump to the head. I'm sure she'll be back before we know it, Utsugi."

Usually, Minoru would automatically get defensive and ask why she'd directed those words at him, but now he simply nodded.

"......Yeah. I'm sure she will."

With another glance at Suu's left shoulder that peeked out from the blanket and a silent, earnest prayer for the quickest recovery possible, Minoru stepped away.

Then something occurred to him, and he looked around. However, there was no one in sight besides the three of them, either inside the ICU or the short hallway.

"Erm...Professor?"

"Hmm?"

"Doesn't Suu have an older brother? Why isn't he here?"

The Professor and Yumiko looked at each other, and both uttered a soft "Well..." at the same time. Minoru's brow furrowed at their strange reaction.

He definitely remembered being told that Suu Komura's older brother was also a Jet Eye and that they'd joined the SFD at the same time. Since apparently the siblings had been taking turns watching Minoru's home when he was away, he was anxious to meet Suu's brother someday so that he could thank him. It was reasonable enough that he never saw him at headquarters, since he was busy with his own duties, but surely they'd allow him to watch over his sister while she was in a coma...?

However, this train of thought was abruptly ended by a few words from the Professor.

"...No, he's here."

"Wh...what? I mean... Where?"

Minoru looked around again, but he still only saw the Professor and Yumiko. Then a possibility finally occurred to him.

"Ah... Does he have the same refraction ability as Suu, maybe...? ...Is he...invisible...?"

Minoru was relatively confident in this conjecture, but this time, it was Yumiko who shook her head.

"Not really. Although I suppose you could say it's a similar sort of ability...or maybe not."

With no idea what to think anymore, Minoru looked back and forth between Professor Riri and Yumiko.

After a few seconds, the Professor cleared her throat as if to shake off some indecision and spoke.

"As a general rule, we usually prefer our members to disclose their abilities at their own discretion, but…Hinako's brother is a special case, so I'll just have to get his consent after the fact… Mikkun, can you see what's on the nurse's cart in the far back of the room there…?"

"Huh…?"

Surprised by the strange question, a bewildered Minoru focused his gaze on the inside of the treatment room.

There was a multistage table with casters on the right side of the room, which was probably the "nurse's cart" that the Professor was referring to. On top of the white surface was an object that was so out of place in the hospital room that Minoru didn't know how he hadn't noticed it before. It was a doll about twenty centimeters in height—a figurine of what looked like a female character from an anime or game, to be precise.

"…Um, the figure…?"

"Mm-hmm. That would be where Shou Komura, SFD code name Spectator, is watching from."

"……"

If this were any other situation, Minoru would probably have assumed that the Professor was just messing with him.

However, Professor Riri didn't seem like the type to make such an absurd joke in front of the comatose Suu, and Yumiko was just as straight-faced standing beside her. Which would mean that this was the truth. The somewhat suggestive figure of an anime girl, who appeared to be wearing armor over a leotard, was Komura's older brother.

"……So is his ability to turn into a figure, or…?"

Unfortunately, or perhaps fortunately, the Professor shook her head at Minoru's hesitant question.

"Not quite. Komsho's consciousness is in that figure, but it's not actually the person himself."

"Kom…"

Minoru was confused for a moment, but then he realized that this was probably the Professor's strange nickname for Suu's older brother, like "Mikkun" and "Hinako." The fact that it seemed to be a mishmash of "Shou" and "Komura" made him sure of it this time.

But that wasn't the concerning part. What exactly did it mean that his consciousness was there, but it wasn't him?

"...So that figure is some sort of medium...?"

Yumiko rapped Minoru briskly on the back, right near his spinal column.

"My, aren't you perceptive."

"I-is that a compliment?"

"Of course it is. Spectator's ability is remote viewing... Though he can't just observe wherever he wants. He can use figures that decorated his room for years to see and hear what's going on wherever they're located."

The Professor added a few words to Yumiko's explanation.

"Incidentally, there's also a figure inside the terminal box attached to the telephone pole in front of your house, Mikkun, and Komsho is watching it even now. If there's anything suspicious sighted, you'll be contacted right away."

"I...see..."

Still astonished, Minoru took another look at the figure in the ICU.

But soon, he came up with another question.

"...Professor, you said before that the Third Eyes manipulate molecules directly in order to manifest their supernatural powers, right? But...how does that explain being able to see a faraway place through a figure's eyes...?"

"An excellent question. But think about DD's powers as the Searcher, for example. He can sense via smell when molecules are being manipulated by Ruby Eyes as far as several kilometers away. There's no exchange of molecules between the Ruby Eye and DD at that moment. My fellow researchers call this phenomenon that allows Third Eyes to manipulate molecules a 'seventh force,' so I think that those sorts of abilities are an effect of this."

"You said it was sort of like telekinesis, right, Professor?"

Minoru nodded, thinking he'd ask Yumiko later why it was called a "seventh force."

"I see... So if DD can smell molecules from far away, it's possible that Mr. Komura can feel the light and air vibrations around the figure...I suppose. I don't get why it has to be figures, but..."

"You'll have to ask Hinako when she wakes up."

With that, the Professor shifted the sleeve of her pink down jacket, reading the time from what looked like a cute kids' wristwatch.

"...Sorry, but our time's just about up. I know it must not feel like we got to visit her at all, since it was only through a window, but..."

"No, it's all right."

Yumiko was the one who answered.

"Even from here, I can tell that Komura is fighting to hang in there, and I'm sure she can feel that we're supporting her, too."

"...I think so, too."

Minoru nodded firmly, and the Professor smiled up at them with a bit of a sparkle in her eyes.

"Yes, you're right. Hinako will return to the SFD soon enough... You'll have to cook her a feast when that happens, Mikkun."

"Of course!"

With an emphatic response, Minoru started to follow the Professor toward the exit of the isolated area.

But just then, he heard a faint vibration sound, and the Professor stopped. Taking her smartphone out from her jacket pocket, she tapped the screen with her thumb. Her brow furrowed, she glanced down at a message from someone, gave a low cry...

"...What's this...?!"

...and turned around on the spot. Passing by Minoru as he hurriedly moved out of the way, she returned to the window of Suu's sickroom and pressed her right hand and forehead against the glass.

"What...what's going on?!"

Without answering Yumiko's question, the Professor kept staring at the bed for a while, then shouted again.

"I-it's true...!"

"Seriously, what happened?!"

"Komsho just texted me to say that Hinako's finger is moving!"

"What...?!" Yumiko and Minoru exclaimed in unison, rushing over to press against the window as well.

Staring at the bed surrounded by monitors, he realized it was true—on Suu's right hand, which was protruding just a little from the white blanket, her index finger was trembling ever so slightly.

"Is...is it just a twitch? Or..."

The Professor quickly shook her head at Yumiko's whisper.

"No, there's regularity in the finger's movements... Hinako is try-ing to tell us something. That movement... Is it Japanese Morse code?! Something about a field...?"

Minoru was impressed by the Professor's immediate recognition of the finger's movement as Morse code, thanks to her speculation ability. However, Yumiko was the first to recognize the contents of the message.

"No, Professor, it's 'inside the shell'!"

At that, the Professor clenched her right hand into a fist.

"Yes, that's it... Hinako is saying she wants to be put inside Mikkun's protective shell!"

Fifteen minutes later, Minoru once again stood in front of the ICU.

He had been made to strip down to his socks and underwear, had his entire body sterilized, and put on a sterile, green clean room suit.

This time, he wasn't here just to pray for Suu Komura's recovery from the other side of the glass. He was going inside to make contact with her.

A doctor, who seemed to know about the SFD and Third Eyes, oper-ated a panel near the sliding doors, causing air to blow out from above the doorframe. This was an air curtain to prevent any contamination and viruses from entering. Then the doctor, who had a name tag on his chest that read "Hongou," looked at Minoru and spoke.

"The door will only be open for two seconds, so please enter as quickly as possible."

"O...okay. I'm ready."

Minoru looked over at the Professor and Yumiko, who were waiting on standby a couple of meters away, then nodded. Dr. Hongou again flicked his fingers along the panel. The instant the door opened with a hiss, Minoru pushed against the air flowing out of the room to step inside. Immediately, the door closed behind him.

The inside of the ICU was quiet and almost odorless, but there was a slight trace of the sweet fragrance that Minoru remembered. He'd smelled it throughout the reconnaissance mission in Minami-Aoyama, when he was carrying Suu Komura on his back.

Minoru first walked straight ahead from the door, approaching the nurse's cart on the right side of the room. There, he gave a little bow to the anime girl figure, through which Shou Komura was apparently watching, before turning to the left.

As soon as he laid eyes on the entirety of the bed, most of which had been hidden from outside of the room, Minoru gasped sharply.

Lying underneath a thin blanket, Suu Komura looked even more fragile than Minoru remembered.

A white bandage was wrapped around her head, and the skin below it was nearly as pale—yet still strikingly beautiful as her eyes lay closed without the slightest flicker of movement. It certainly looked as though she was still comatose, but the index finger of her right hand, jutting out from under the blanket, occasionally twitched faintly. Most likely, she had used up all her strength sending the Morse code message before and was desperately trying to convey something despite her exhaustion.

"……Suu."

When Minoru spoke to her quietly, the movement of her finger seemed to become just a bit stronger.

There was no point in simply standing there wasting time. Gathering his resolve, Minoru approached the bed and gently grasped her right hand with his left.

For a moment, the coolness of her smooth skin made him falter a little. But he could still feel Suu's will to live somewhere beneath that coldness.

Still holding her hand, Minoru sat on the bed with his left knee. Thinking of how the Professor, Yumiko, the doctor, and Suu's brother were all watching threatened to overwhelm him with embarrassment, but this was no time for being distracted. He pulled away the blanket, folded it up, and placed it on the nearby cart, exposing Suu's body, which was clad only in a simple hospital gown.

The IV line, the electrodes of the ECG monitor, and so on had already been removed by Dr. Hongou, but the cannula still in her left arm looked awfully painful. Minoru felt nervous about putting all his weight on such a frail body, but even with her serious injuries, she should still have the enhanced healing abilities granted by the Third Eye. He put his right hand over Suu's as well despite his cast, lined his feet up with hers, and carefully positioned himself to cover her body.

Finally, he put his head on the pillow next to Suu's right ear and let the strength go out of his body. However, he still couldn't relax his mental tension.

Minoru didn't want to doubt that Suu's Morse code message, "inside the shell," meant that she wanted to be put inside Minoru's protective barrier. However, if he failed at bringing her inside, her body would suffer a powerful shock. Even a novice like Minoru knew that this would have a traumatic effect on her brain, since she'd just had decompression surgery performed on her so recently.

Professor Riri Isa and Dr. Hongou understood this danger but chose to prioritize Suu's wishes. This was also a show of faith in Minoru. He had to live up to their expectations—but the thought was making his breathing shallow and his limbs cold.

Then...

He felt the fingers of Suu's right hand, grasped in his left hand, starting to move again. They had been so cold not long ago, but now they were rather warm.

Encouraged by the gentle warmth and trembling of her hands, Minoru concentrated hard, taking a deep breath of the sweet-scented air. Gathering as much air as he could, he put pressure on the Third Eye embedded in his breastbone.

Minoru's ability as the Isolator, his protective shell, activated, tinting his field of vision blue.

Only when all sound had disappeared did he realize that the treatment room, which had seemed so quiet, had been full of the noise of operating machinery. In its place was a mysterious low hum that sounded as if it was coming from far away. And beneath that, the soft sound of Suu Komura's breathing.

Suu's body, pressed close to Minoru's, was floating about two centimeters above the sheets and pillow. He'd succeeded in bringing her into the shell.

But that was all. He kept waiting, but there was no sign that Suu would wake up.

The Professor had warned him before he'd entered the room of the possibility that nothing would happen. It might just be her muddled consciousness wishing for that, and if anything, the odds of something happening were much lower.

It made sense. Minoru's ability could only create an invisible barrier around his body to render him invulnerable. It was still a mystery how the shell could stop radiant heat, or electromagnetic waves, while allowing visible light through, or how there was still enough air to breathe despite it being an airtight space, but at the very least it was clear that it had no heightened healing powers or anything like that.

And yet.

Five days ago, when they first tested Minoru's ability to bring Suu into the shell in his room, she seemed to like it inside. If this would help Suu feel even a little more at ease during her desperate battle, he would gladly continue for minutes or even hours.

"......Suu?"

Minoru felt the bandage over her right ear as he whispered to her.

"You said something before you got onto the helicopter, didn't you? That I'm the hope of all the Jet Eyes...no, everyone who has a Third Eye. To be honest, I don't believe that at all. And I don't know if I'll ever change... All this time, I've lived my life trying to avoid getting close to or involved with anyone. Because I couldn't bear to make any more unhappy, painful memories. I was afraid that that sort of thing would combine with my memories of that night...the night when my parents and older sister were killed...and start to take over my mind completely."

As he spoke, scenes from the night he was describing flickered in the back of his mind.

His sister Wakaba's smile as she hid Minoru in the storage space under the floor of the pantry. And her last words.

Don't worry. I'll protect you, Mii.

Wakaba, who was only eleven years old at the time, had kept her promise. In order to defend the eight-year-old Minoru, she stood against the murderer who had invaded their home, and she lost her life in the process.

If only...if only Minoru had been able to go out and help his sister instead of trembling in the storage space below the floor. Even if they couldn't take on the murderer directly, perhaps Minoru could have distracted him long enough for both his sister and himself to escape, instead of only Minoru...

Of course, it was just as likely that he would have been caught by the criminal and killed along with his sister. But maybe that would have been better than being the sole surviving family member. Though these thoughts betrayed Wakaba's determination and willingness to die to protect him, he still couldn't help but feel this way, no matter how he tried.

"...I've tried so hard to seal the memories of that night away in the bottom of my heart. But I couldn't do it... Every time something bad happens, I remember it and feel so distraught... I've even tried to go to where my sister is, more than once. But...since the Third Eye became part of my body, I met Yumiko, DD, Oli-V, the Professor...and you, Suu... I've finally realized that even I can do something for the sake of others. Of course, that's the power that the Third Eye gave me, not my own strength. And that power might disappear someday. But I think, if there's anything I can do now... If I can help someone, I want to do it... I want to stand up against evil, like my older sister did back then. So..."

He didn't know if his words were reaching Suu at all. Nevertheless, Minoru earnestly kept trying to put his feelings into words.

"......So I'll believe what you told me, Suu. I'll do my best to become someone's hope. And I need your strength for that, Suu... I need you."

Minoru wanted to hug Suu tightly to convey all his thoughts and emotions, but the protective shell's shape would adjust to match his posture. If he moved both arms now, he would force Suu's unconscious body to move.

So instead, he clasped both her hands tightly as he spoke.

"Suu, please come back. To the SFD...to us."

At the same time, he prayed with all his might, deep in his heart. Just as he had when he broke out of Liquidizer's concrete trap on the first floor of the Syndicate safe house.

Please, Wakaa...my sister. If you're still looking over me...please save this person, the person who saved my life.

There was no reason to believe that anything would happen.

But in that moment, Minoru felt something.

Near the top of his head, something was moving. It wasn't outside the protective shell. But somehow, somewhere far away from the two-centimeter space of the shell, something was coming closer.

Something with no physical substance, yet warm beyond compare, touched Minoru's and Suu's heads for an instant, then quickly moved away. Then it made contact again, a little longer this time, and the third time it stayed there. It was as if a young child was placing a hand on an unknown something, trying to ascertain its existence...

Then the "hand" permeated inside Suu's head.

At the same time, Minoru thought he heard something. Something mingling with the rhythmic bass sound that was always present inside the shell, like music…or words.

Abruptly, Suu's body quivered. Near Minoru's ear, he heard the sound of a deep breath. He fought desperately against the reflex to cancel the shell. Because he knew instinctively that whatever was touching Suu's head was not a bad thing by any means.

An unbelievably long moment passed, and the warm presence pulled away from Suu, moved farther off—and vanished.

After several deep breaths, Minoru held his breath again and canceled the protective shell.

Their bodies fell just a little, sinking into the bed. Minoru hurriedly pulled back and looked at Suu's face.

There was no change. The bandages were still tightly wrapped around her head, of course, and her cheeks were pale as ever, her eyes still closed.

Was it all in his mind? The feeling that something had touched their heads, the mysterious voice, the trembling of Suu's body, the change in her breathing?

"……Suu…," Minoru murmured in a choked voice.

Then, in his left hand, he felt her small right hand move stiffly.

Her five fingers spread open, entwined with Minoru's, and grasped his hand.

Her long eyelashes began to tremble, lifting little by little.

Her eyes flickered twice. Then once more, slowly. Finally, two violet eyes the color of dawn looked into Minoru's from mere centimeters away.

Her small lips moved, and a nearly soundless whisper reached Minoru's ears.

"……I'm back, Minoru."

4

As he filled his lungs with cold air, Ryuu Mikawa felt a sharp pain from his left shoulder to the pit of his stomach.

Enduring the pain, Mikawa pursed his lips and blew a puff of air.

The long, thin stream of air glittered cold and white, coiling around the ice pillar before his eyes. This was Mikawa's power as the Ruby Eye Trancer, which allowed him to freeze the moisture in the air instantly.

The cold air turned into frost, then ice, adding another layer of thickness to the semitransparent pillar of ice hardened around OO.

His work finished, Mikawa trod across the frosted floor, approaching the pillar. Removing the Gore-Tex-lined glove from his right hand so that only a thin inner glove covered it, Mikawa pressed that hand against the icy pillar. He would have preferred to touch it with his bare hand, but if he did that in this thirty-degree-below-zero room, the palm of his hand would stick to the surface, and he'd have to use his ability to melt some of the ice he'd worked so hard to build up in order to free it.

Still, Mikawa could definitely feel OO's presence through the polyester fiber. After stroking the ice over and over, he turned his back to it and leaned against the pillar.

This was deep inside an antique F2 cold-storage warehouse in Tokai 6-chome, Oka district, specifically the southern part of Ooi Futo Park. The measurement of cold-storage temperatures was divided into seven categories, ranging from C3, meaning anything below ten degrees Celsius, to F4, anything below negative fifty degrees. The warehouse was used mostly to store meat, frozen food, ice cream, and so on.

Mikawa had known about all this since he was in elementary school. His father had worked in the frozen-storage division of a major distribution company, albeit different from the one that owned this particular storehouse.

And so, six years ago—in the winter of his fourth year in elementary school—when he found a key on the side of a road near this storehouse, he knew exactly where it could be used. There was a plastic tag attached to the key with the business name and warehouse designation.

The friend who was with him at the time, OO, had suggested that they turn it over to the police, but Mikawa insisted on using it to check out the warehouse instead. More than anything, he wanted to see the ultra-low-temperature world in which his father worked.

Mikawa managed to convince the reluctant OO, and the following Sunday, they donned their thickest clothes and headed to the cold-storage warehouse indicated on the plate. Because it was midwinter, there was nothing suspicious about their appearance.

The frozen food–storage warehouses often took the day off on Sundays, since the city market was closed then. There was only one security guard at the main gate of the warehouse, which they avoided easily by creeping through the shrubbery that surrounded the grounds. The key Mikawa had picked up was for the break room on the side of the storehouse, not the truck entrance, but they were still able to enter the cold-storage warehouse through the double doors inside.

For Mikawa and OO, who were both born and raised in Tokyo, seeing the negative-thirty-degree space for the first time was like entering a frozen area from an anime or video game. Above them, the high racks stacked with boxes were all covered in pure-white frost, and their exhaled breath gleamed in the air. That day, they were only able to handle the cold for a few minutes before bursting back outside through the double doors. Running along the road in the early afternoon, Mikawa and OO both laughed aloud.

That single moment from that day might have been the very brightest memory in Mikawa's sixteen years…

"Hmm. So this is your little nest, is it, boy?"

Mikawa's eyes widened.

He knew he'd been alone when he came in, but now a woman in a long fur coat stood inside the cold-storage warehouse. She was tall and slender, with her long hair gathered up in a twist bun above her cool, beautiful face. This was none other than Liquidizer, a veteran Ruby Eye from the Syndicate.

Standing up shakily, Mikawa addressed her hoarsely.

"…Master… Why are you here…?"

A bewitching smile spread across his former teacher's ruby lips.

"Oh, please. As if I wouldn't know about your little hideout?"

"But… How did you get in? You didn't melt the door, did you?"

As a response, Liquidizer fished around in her coat pocket, pulling out a brand-new key in her leather-gloved right hand and giving it a little shake.

"I wouldn't resort to such a violent act. I simply had a key made while you were groaning over your injuries, boy."

"......I see."

Mikawa would've liked to shoot her a wry smile, but it was already taking all his effort just to hide his intense nervousness.

Ever since he'd picked it up six years ago, Mikawa had constantly carried that key on his person as if bound to it. Quite literally, since it was always on a thin but strong titanium chain attached to a ring piercing on his left hip via a key ring. The only way to remove the key without cutting the chain would be to dismantle the segment ring–style body piercing, but that would be absolutely impossible to do without Mikawa noticing, even if he was asleep.

Of course, he'd removed the plate with the company name that had been attached to the key and attached six dummy keys to the key ring, just in case. And yet, Liquidizer had discovered this warehouse without a problem and even went so far as to have a copy of the key made.

"But how on earth did you...?"

Mikawa trailed off as a possibility occurred to him and quickly pulled the key ring out of the left pocket of his jeans. Yanking off the inner glove from his left hand with his teeth, he traced the titanium chain connected to the skin of his left hip with a fingertip. Then, somewhere in the middle of the chain, he noticed that one of the rings was warped ever so slightly.

".........Wow, you got me good. You must've melted the chain while I was sleeping, made off with the key, had a copy made, then liquefied it back on, right?"

"*Exactement.*"

Answering in flawless French, Liquidizer removed her left glove like Mikawa. Then she tossed the key from her right hand to her left, and instantly it turned to silver droplets of liquid, which hardened again due to the low temperature and fell to the floor as countless little metal balls. Liquidizer had melted the stainless steel key with her liquefaction ability. Again, she spoke with a smirk.

"But I suppose I don't need it anymore."

Unable to guess at the meaning of her words, Mikawa stared bluntly at his former master as he returned the key to his pocket and slipped his hand back into the inner glove.

Liquidizer, on the other hand, simply looked around the warehouse with an utterly unconcerned gesture before she continued.

"We Ruby Eyes do love to make nests, but yours is really quite a unique case, boy."

"……"

Ignoring Mikawa's lack of response, Liquidizer stepped closer, her long black boots pressing into the frost on the floor.

"…Or is this not a nest but a grave? For that poor girl covered in ice over there…?"

"Don't come any closer, please."

On hearing Mikawa's low voice, Liquidizer stopped with a smile.

If there was any chance that Liquidizer intended to melt the pillar of ice in which OO slept, he would have to fight her—even if she was a fellow Ruby Eye and his former teacher.

He knew he had little chance of winning. All the moisture in this warehouse was in a frozen state, and if Mikawa were to try to fight her with his ability, the most he could do was instantly alter that into steam. However, he absolutely couldn't raise the temperature of this place. No matter what.

Even without that constraint, Mikawa didn't think that he could win in a real battle against his old master.

Frankly, Ryuu Mikawa's ability as the Trancer was only to manipulate the thermal vibrations of water molecules. Increasing the frequency would weaken the bond between molecules, changing ice to water, then water to steam. If the frequency was lowered, the opposite phenomenon would occur. In other words, all Mikawa could really control was the hydrogen bonds of water molecules.

However, Liquidizer, whose real name he still didn't know, had control over the bonds of all molecules. Aside from hydrogen bonds, this also included van der Waals forces, ionic bonds, covalent bonds, and metal bonds, all of which she could weaken to convert solids into liquids. Even the peptide bonds of proteins were no exception: The instant her hand made contact, the Liquidizer could turn a human body into a horrific soup.

The only substances that she couldn't liquefy were, of course, liquid, gas, and energy with no physical form.

In the battle at Minami-Aoyama, Liquidizer had fought a boy with ash-colored hair who was a member of the Jet Eye group and had broken two fingers on her right hand when she attempted to liquefy his mysterious protection field. On top of that, she had been taken down by a high-powered stun gun wielded by a girl with an accelerating ability.

It had only been three days since then, yet nothing about Liquidizer's appearance or demeanor indicated any hint of injury. However, judging by the fact that she hadn't removed the glove on her right hand, her bone fractures probably hadn't healed, and she most likely had burns left where her body had been exposed to the high-ampere current.

Even in that state, she had liquefied the ground itself to escape to an underground sewage tunnel in order to save Mikawa, who had suffered even more serious injuries. She had put aside her strong pride to carry the unconscious Mikawa through kilometers of sewage and bring him to the Syndicate's safe house in Gotanda.

Remembering that, Mikawa felt the wounds in his chest begin to ache again.

Unconsciously grimacing, Mikawa repeated himself.

"…Don't come any closer, please. I don't want to fight you."

Still smiling, Liquidizer tilted her head slightly.

"Oh my. I didn't know you could make a face like that, boy. Usually, you look as though you could hardly care less if you lived or died."

"…It's not that I'm afraid of dying, I just don't want to die here. If I die, my Third Eye will burst out of me and open up a huge hole in the roof of this warehouse. Then the ice inside would melt away…"

"Hmm. I see."

Looking back at Mikawa, Liquidizer's smile faded into a serious expression.

"Does that mean you'd fight me as long as it's somewhere else?"

"……"

Unable to respond immediately, Mikawa searched his heart.

His claim that he wasn't afraid to die was no lie. Six years ago, when OO sank into eternal sleep in this warehouse… No, to be more precise, it was exactly a year later, the instant that he knew she would never wake up, that Mikawa lost his reason for living. He stopped going to school in his second semester of middle school, but instead of shutting himself up at home, he spent his days gazing at the water in places like the Tokyo-Yokohama Canal and Tokyo Bay. He didn't go to high school, either.

If he hadn't reached out his hand toward the red sphere that descended from the sky four months ago, Mikawa would probably be engulfed in ice with OO in this very warehouse right now.

But now Mikawa knew. That there were still enormous mysteries in this world.

And he thought. That perhaps if he used the phase transition power the sphere had given him, he could wake OO.

Even if it was impossible, Mikawa had an important goal now...a dream that he wanted to achieve. So even if he wasn't afraid to die here, he still preferred to live.

"...Are you familiar with the Snowball Earth hypothesis?"

Liquidizer blinked at Mikawa's sudden question.

"I believe I've heard of it. Something to do with the whole planet freezing over...?"

"Global glaciation, yes. I'm not surprised you're familiar... It refers to an ice age so intense that the entire earth would be covered in ice. In the end, it's still just a hypothesis, but there are scholars who assert that it actually happened hundreds of millions of years ago. I want to see that."

"See it? In reality, you mean? Are you saying you want to freeze the entire planet?"

Liquidizer's eyes widened, and Mikawa nodded seriously.

"That's right. You said the Syndicate's ultimate goal is the extinction of the entire human race, but that's no easy task, right? We certainly can't kill them all one by one. But if Snowball Earth were to be realized, humanity wouldn't be able to survive. I think it's worth considering as a means for that."

He had never voiced these words aloud before. He had planned on proposing it directly to whatever Ruby Eye was the leader of the Syndicate once he gained the organization's trust.

He didn't particularly care about gaining status in the Syndicate. He just wanted to see it with his own eyes: the entire planet turned white with frost.

Even after Mikawa stopped speaking, Liquidizer remained silent for several more seconds.

"......Pfft..."

Suddenly, a tiny snicker escaped from her crimson-tinted lips.

"Heh...ah-ha-ha, ah-ha-ha-ha..."

With each peal of laughter, a puff of white floated into the air.

Mikawa would normally have suspected that she was mocking him. But there was something about the strangely childish, earnest undertone of her laughter that suggested otherwise.

After a while of this, Liquidizer raised her right hand as if in apology and caught her breath. Finally, she wiped a tear from the corner of her eye, snapping the frozen bead with her finger.

"...Whew... I apologize for laughing like that."

"It's all right... I mean, it is a pretty ridiculous idea."

"It certainly is. However, I don't dislike it. Especially not compared to our fellows like Norma, who kill people one by one, week after week."

Mikawa felt a bit embarrassed at her words.

Global glaciation was certainly a grandiose dream, but at present, Mikawa was no better than Norma, since he committed such petty murder once a month. And rather than killing people he wanted to kill, he was simply giving in to the violent impulses of the Ruby Eye and the rush of intoxication after committing such indiscriminate murder. He was no better than an addict.

It was only six days ago that he froze the downhill slope on the street in Aoyama, sending a huge trailer into the Akasaka intersection and killing seven people. The Ruby Eye inside his body was content for now, but after two weeks or so, he would be overwhelmed with a thirst-like sensation that could only be quenched by killing another person at the end of the month.

"...What choice do we have about that? If you don't kill people, the Ruby Eye will take over your mind and go on a rampage."

When Mikawa absentmindedly muttered these words as if to defend his colleague, Liquidizer gave another smile—this time with the usual subdued irony.

"Heh, true enough. But going about killing haphazardly like Biter won't do, either; we're not animals. Even if we must kill, there's still the matter of maintaining one's dignity, is there not?"

"Dignity...? Do you mean aesthetically? Like the way Igniter killed people who were generating excessive amounts of CO_2?"

"Hmm, not exactly, but…well, close enough. At the very least, I intend to choose the people I kill quite strictly. Which means I have no intention of doing anything to you here. Or the princess behind you, either."

At those words, Mikawa let out a little sigh of relief. Only now that the tension was leaving his body did he realize that his neck and shoulders had stiffened without his noticing.

Although he doubted that Liquidizer was feeling the same relief, she did let out a rather adorable sneeze and belatedly start rubbing her arms.

"At any rate, it's awfully cold in here."

"Well, yes. It's negative thirty degrees."

"Even if Ruby Eyes don't catch colds, we'll end up with frostbite if we stand around in here for too long. Would you like to come and get something warm to eat?"

"……I-I'm not particularly hungry…"

"Aren't you wondering why I'm here? I came to talk to you about something that can't be discussed over the phone. Come on, then, boy."

With that, she turned and walked toward the exit.

After one last look at the pillar of ice, Mikawa whispered, "I'll be back" to OO sleeping inside and followed his former master.

At the exit, he moved ahead of her and held the heavy double doors open. Once his former teacher passed, he left as well, promptly locking the doors behind him.

The small break room was empty, of course, since it was a holiday. Mikawa picked up the shoulder bag he'd left on the old sofa. As Liquidizer approached the exit to the outside, she paused and closed her eyes as if searching for something. A high-class Ruby Eye like her could detect an enemy's presence even through a door, but Mikawa wasn't that powerful yet.

Apparently satisfied, Liquidizer opened the door herself.

As he followed his former teacher outside, the cool January air felt somewhat warm.

Leaving Tokai 6-chome and the cold-storage warehouses behind, Liquidizer drove the pair in a Suzuki Swift to Odaiba, where they entered an *okonomiyaki* shop in Aqua City. The shop was of Liquidizer's choosing, not Mikawa's.

Mikawa ordered salted cabbage, minced cucumbers, oysters, and beef with green onions, then lightly clinked his mug of oolong tea against his former teacher's. She had removed her long coat, revealing an ivory mohair knit sweater.

With the first sip, he immediately thought the ice was of poor quality, but he was in no position to express this dissatisfaction. This was his first time dining out with Liquidizer.

When Mikawa first became a Third Eye host, he'd been unable to handle the life of a cold-blooded murderer; his first kill had been on September 16 of last year. He had used his ability on two shady men who were wandering the streets on a drizzly evening and approached him to demand some money.

At the time, he'd barely had enough power to cover someone's face with ice, never mind encasing their entire body; so, on the news the next day, it was reported that the men had suffocated when their respiratory tracts became blocked up with ice, not that they'd frozen to death. There were no witnesses, but since the town was teeming with cameras, Mikawa was sure the police would come to arrest him at any moment.

However, it wasn't a police officer who rang the doorbell of his apartment two days later but the woman who now sat across from him, munching away on some minced cucumber.

Mikawa had been infected with a Third Eye on September 7. It was September 18 when Liquidizer made contact with him. Apparently, the Third Eyes hadn't dropped on Tokyo all at once but over a span of about five days at most, and yet, this meant that the Ruby Eye organization, the Syndicate, already existed only about ten days later. The SFD, a Jet Eye group, was apparently made in early October, so it seemed strange that this group had been formed more than half a month sooner than that. And Mikawa still didn't know how Liquidizer had found him before the police.

Mikawa—though he'd gone by a different name at the time—had been living on his own due to family circumstances since he finished middle school, though he'd only attended about half the time. Liquidizer was the person who gave him information about the Third Eyes and taught him how to live while diffusing his murderous impulses.

On her recommendation, he moved out of his apartment, changed his name to Ryuu Mikawa, and occupied a room the Syndicate had prepared for him on September 22. From that point onward, his combat training using his abilities and firearms began, and on the evening of

October 5, a night he would never forget, Mikawa participated in a Syndicate mission for the first time. This was also the first time that he met his archenemy at the SFD, Divider.

"Thanks for waitiiing! Here are your oysters and beef with green onions!"

The waitress's energetic voice interrupted Mikawa's reminiscing.

She offered to make the *okonomiyaki* for them, but Liquidizer declined with a brilliant smile. As soon as the waitress left, looking a little disappointed, the smile vanished from Liquidizer's face as she whispered to Mikawa.

"Why would we want someone else to do the grilling for us when there's a hot plate at the table for that very purpose?"

"Y-yeah… I guess you're right."

Mikawa nodded and picked up the bowl of beef with green onions he'd ordered.

At that moment, he suddenly wondered how many years it had been since he last made the grilled pancake, but he couldn't remember. He hadn't even eaten out with anyone since elementary school.

"Er, so, you mix this together, right?" Mikawa asked in a small voice as he stared at the heap of ingredients in the small metal bowl, and his former master nodded gravely.

"That's right."

"But the bowl is so small… Why don't they use a bigger one?"

"There's a very good reason for its size, boy."

"What do you mean?"

"It deliberately makes it harder to mix. If you stir the batter too much, excess gluten will be produced, and then what do you think happens?"

"Erm……"

Resisting the urge to ask whether a lesson was really necessary right now, Mikawa instead thought hard about the answer.

He had studied the science of water's phase transitions and molecular bonds out of necessity, but wheat proteins were outside Mikawa's wheelhouse. But if he remembered correctly, kneading the dough for things like bread and udon was meant to produce gluten, so…

"…It gets sticky?"

Mikawa's shot-in-the-dark response made Liquidizer's smile widen a little.

"*Bonne réponse.* And here is your reward."

Liquidizer used a spoon to scoop one oyster from her bowl and transfer it to Mikawa's.

"Th-thanks... Although I feel like that just made it a little harder to mix."

"But it'll be all the tastier for it, no? ...If too much gluten is produced in the batter, it won't get fluffy when you cook it. This much should be plenty."

With that, Liquidizer stirred deftly with her spoon, revolving the heap of ingredients in the bowl just twice. Mikawa tried to imitate her movement, but the batter spilled over the edge of the bowl a bit. His instinct was to harden it with a concentrated breath, but he couldn't go using his powers here, so he resisted the urge.

"...You know, every time I go out for *okonomiyaki*, it gets me thinking."

Liquidizer spoke up abruptly as she gazed at her bowl.

"Oh? About what?"

"I can't help but wonder... What would it taste like if I liquefied the contents of this bowl into a perfectly homogeneous liquid and cooked it?"

"Wh...what?"

"Of course, you'd lose the mouthfeel of the ingredients, but it would completely eradicate the gluten that's inevitably produced no matter how carefully you stir, right? If you grilled that, I can only imagine that it would produce the ultimate fluffy *okonomiyaki*..."

Liquidizer gazed intently at the bowl as she spoke, so Mikawa rapidly shook his head.

"Y-you really shouldn't use your ability in a place like this, master. What if one of the black ones was nearby?"

"I know, I know. It's just a thought."

With that rather petulant response, Liquidizer added some oil to the hot plate and effortlessly poured the contents of the bowl onto it. Steam rose from the plate with a sizzling sound. After expertly adjusting its shape and thickness with a spoon, Liquidizer made no further movement to touch the cooking *okonomiyaki*.

"......Let's try it at the safe house sometime, then."

Mikawa poured his own batter onto the hot plate and crinkled his face up in concentration as he spoke, and his former master looked up and grinned.

"An excellent idea... Hey! Are you insane? Don't push the batter around so much. The trick to grilling things like this is to touch it as little as possible while it cooks."

"...'Insane'...?"

My own father never even talked to me like that, Mikawa thought, but he kept that to himself as he put the spoon down in the empty bowl.

After he heaved a little sigh and took another sip of his oolong tea, Mikawa finally remembered why they'd come here.

"...So, master, what did you need to talk about that we couldn't discuss on the phone?"

"Oh yes..."

Liquidizer looked up from the hot plate and quickly cast her eyes around the room.

It was still early for dinner, but since it was New Year's, the restaurant was already bustling with families at most of the tables. As long as they spoke at a low volume barely audible to their enhanced Ruby Eye hearing, it would be impossible for anyone at the nearby tables to listen in.

Or so Mikawa thought. But nonetheless, Liquidizer slid over on the oblong sofa she was sitting on and patted the now-empty space.

"Come over here, boy."

"Uh...a-all right."

Trying to argue with her over this would be a waste of time, so Mikawa meekly obeyed.

As he sat down next to Liquidizer, he was struck by the fresh, woodsy scent of her perfume.

It was then that Mikawa finally thought to wonder what his and Liquidizer's relationship must look like to the people around them. They certainly couldn't be mistaken for a couple, given the contrast between Liquidizer's sharp, expensive-looking outfit and accessories and Mikawa's secondhand zip-up coat worn over a faded T-shirt. Brother and sister, perhaps, or a boss and a part-time worker... At the very least, it was doubtful that anyone would suspect that they were murderers with supernatural powers.

"You're aware that the Keihinjima hideout in Oomisoka was attacked, correct?"

Mikawa felt his skin go cold for a moment at the sudden whisper.

"Y…yes. I heard while I was being treated."

He nodded, matching her low volume.

"At first, all I was told was that it was a warehouse near Ooi Futo… I was terrified that something had happened to the cold-storage warehouse."

"My apologies. The hideout in question was being used to scout out Haneda Airport. That's probably why they went after it so aggressively… But as of today, we finally have a damage report."

"They shot the place up with a machine gun from a helicopter, right? How many of our people died?"

As Mikawa's teacher, Liquidizer had repeatedly told him that a single handgun was more powerful than just about any attack-type Third Eye ability. So if a large-caliber machine gun was brought into the equation, there were probably very few Ruby Eyes who could counteract it, if any. Mikawa doubted that even he himself could survive a situation like that, unless there was heavy rain and he was able to make a preemptive strike. Liquidizer, whose power could liquefy even machine-gun bullets, might be the only one who would stand a chance.

He only knew a few other Syndicate members' faces besides Liquidizer's, but Mikawa's stomach still fluttered as he awaited a response. However…

"Zero."

"What…?"

"There were no casualties. The only physical losses were some equipment we'd been stockpiling for recon, a laptop used for communication, and a few beds and such. Some information may have been leaked from the PC, though…"

"Is that all…? Judging by your face, I was sure someone had died."

Mikawa breathed a little sigh. Then Liquidizer's right hand moved in a flash.

With the silver spatula somehow already grasped in her hand, Liquidizer expertly flipped the two *okonomiyaki*, which were starting to give off a delicious smell.

Mikawa wondered if her intense look had just been because she was watching for the perfect moment to flip the cakes, but her expression didn't change when she put the spatula down.

"Well, yes, some did. Six people, to be precise."

"What…!"

"But that was on their side, not ours."

"……!!"

Mikawa sat up in shock, more alarmed by this news than he expected.

"Six…Jet Eyes? Wouldn't that mean all of them…?"

His constant rival Divider, the stun gun–wielding Accelerator, the boy in that protective force field…all of them were dead?

Mikawa was shocked for a few seconds, then thought again.

"…No, that can't be. All of them were in a sorry state after our fight on New Year's Eve. I can't imagine they would participate in another mission just a few hours later…"

"Yes, I agree. I thought that was strange, too, so I pressed for more information, and now we finally have it. It seems that the black agents who died at Keihinjima belonged to a different group, not the usual SFD lot."

"A different group… Does that mean there's a new team of Jet Eyes unrelated to Divider and the others…?"

"That's right. And they belonged to the Self-Defense Forces, at that… It certainly explains why an attack helicopter would show up."

"No way…"

The strange sense of relief that had bubbled up when he learned that Divider and the others were alive disappeared in an instant.

"The Self-Defense Forces…? So these were soldiers with Third Eye abilities…?"

"We still don't know for sure whether all six were actually Jet Eyes. But they were certainly armed to the teeth. It seems they were even outfitted with newly developed combat suits."

"…Sounds like they mean business."

"Well, the number of people that Syndicate Ruby Eyes have killed in the Kanto region is easily over a hundred as of last month. And if you count the prey of independent Ruby Eyes like Biter, that's nearly two hundred people. Clearly, that's enough to motivate the government a smidge."

"…You don't think that 'smidge' is enough to wipe out the entire Syndicate, do you?"

"I doubt that, no?"

With that casual remark, Liquidizer reached for the tin can on the table. Brushing the thick sauce onto the apparently finished *okonomiyaki*, she turned back toward Mikawa. "Mayonnaise?" she asked.

"Erm…yes, please."

"*D'accord.*"

Liquidizer drew zigzag lines of the thick, white mayonnaise across the top of the *okonomiyaki*, then sprinkled bonito flakes and seaweed over them. "Go on, then."

As soon as the scent of the sauce sizzling on the hot plate reached Mikawa's nose, he realized just how hungry he was. In the past, he'd been a rather light eater, but that wouldn't be enough to compensate for the high-energy consumption of his current Third Eye–enhanced body. Though he was still concerned about their conversation, he started by cutting off a large slice of the beef and green onion *okonomiyaki* with the spatula and moving it to his plate, then used chopsticks to bring a piece to his mouth.

This restaurant was only a chain in a shopping mall, but there was a certain sense of stability to that, too. The *okonomiyaki*, his first in longer than he could remember, was so delicious that he polished off his first slice in no time at all.

"…It really is fluffy. I had no idea that there was such an important trick to mixing the batter."

"Right? And the cooking is important, too. The chance to eat *okonomiyaki* I've cooked is an awfully rare commodity, you know."

In profile, Liquidizer's proud expression made her look as if she'd aged backward from somewhere in her mid-twenties to the same age as Mikawa. He blinked a few times.

In the back of his mind, he remembered her appearance when they'd met up at the factory in Minami-Aoyama: a school uniform, dark glasses, and braided hair. At the time, he'd asked her whether that was a disguise or her real appearance, but she simply dodged the question.

He wondered whether he should ask again, but she didn't give him a chance.

"The problem is, we have no idea who in our group killed the six members of the SDF's little SWAT team."

Mikawa swallowed this new information along with the *okonomiyaki*.

"…We don't know…?"

"That's right. The hideout in Keihinjima was intended for an attack on the government officials' personal aircraft, but that was planned for much, much later...near the end of our plan to wipe out humanity. So there were no members regularly stationed at that warehouse—it should have been unmanned on the day of the attack."

The plans she referred to certainly caught Mikawa's attention, but for now he decided to keep that in the back of his mind and carry on the current conversation.

"...But since they were at a Syndicate hideout, it must have been a member, right? And killing six of those super-soldiers would've been a pretty tall order. Why wouldn't they just come forward?"

"I know I would. You'd probably get a pretty hefty bonus, for one thing... But even after three days, no one has taken responsibility. In fact, the executives have been asking members face-to-face if they did it, and so far, everyone has denied it."

As she spoke, Liquidizer somehow finished off a quarter of the oyster *okonomiyaki* with both speed and elegance, then cut off another slice and put it on Mikawa's plate.

"Let me try yours, too."

"S-sure."

Mikawa cut off a large slice of the beef and onion, moving it to his former master's plate. Her chopsticks moved in the blink of an eye, making short work of the piece on her plate.

"Hmm...they'd be passing ingredients for stew, I suppose. Certainly, not on the level of the *suji modanyaki* in Marunouchi."

"Wh-what on earth is that?"

"*Okonomiyaki* topped with yakisoba and egg. It's fluffalicious."

"Wh...what?"

"I'll take you there next time... Anyway, that brings us to the main topic of the day."

Finishing her cup of oolong tea, Liquidizer looked into Mikawa's face from just centimeters away.

"Was it you at the Keihinjima hideout, boy?"

"Huh?!" Mikawa shouted without thinking, then looked around in a panic.

Fortunately, neither the staff nor the customers seemed to be paying them any mind. Dropping his volume, he continued.

"O-of course not. I mean, weren't you carrying me at the time because of my injuries? I wasn't even conscious."

"Fair enough... Do you know which member might've been there, then?"

This must be the main question.

Taking a deep breath, Mikawa shook his head emphatically.

"I don't know. You can even have that Peeping Tom Empathizer scan my memories if you want."

Empathizer was one of the few Ruby Eyes whose name and face were known to Mikawa. Liquidizer shrugged lightly at this.

"That won't be necessary. I can tell for myself whether you're lying, boy. And I knew from the start that it couldn't be you anyway."

"...Then why did you bring me out to eat and everything...?"

"Orders from the top. All the mentors have been told to speak to the members they looked after directly about it."

"That's a pretty high-strung, roundabout way of doing things for the Syndicate. Usually they're so hands-off that it's almost alarming."

"...Most likely, they intend to use Empathizer if nobody comes forward at this rate. It would be too difficult to have Empathizer examine the memories of every single member from that night, but it's easy enough to just double-check the memory of when they were asked about it."

"...So he might take a look inside my head after all, then."

Mikawa chewed his lip a little.

If it was only the memory of being quizzed by Liquidizer just now, it would be mildly uncomfortable at worst. However, he definitely didn't want anyone looking at the memory of an hour ago, in the cold-storage warehouse. If Empathizer saw that, Mikawa would have to kill him.

"No need to look so distressed."

Mikawa stiffened when he felt the sudden whisper at his left ear.

Placing her hand on Mikawa's right shoulder, Liquidizer brought her face even closer to his. At this rate, they'd draw the attention of others even if they couldn't hear a thing.

But his former master didn't seem to care about that as she continued to speak.

"If by any chance you do end up being scanned, I'll be there with you. I won't let him look at any more memories than necessary."

At these words, Mikawa finally understood Liquidizer's intentions. At the same time, for whatever reason, he felt a prickling pain deep in his chest.

"...I see... So that's why you took me all the way to Odaiba instead of asking me at the warehouse. You were buying time to make sure Empathizer couldn't go all the way back to that point so easily."

"Well, that's not the only reason. The more information that's present in a memory, the harder it is for Empathizer to scan further back. The crowds in Odaiba and the taste and smell of *okonomiyaki* should make for a sizable challenge, wouldn't you agree?"

"...Most definitely."

Nodding, Mikawa opened his mouth wide and popped in the piece of oyster *okonomiyaki* that Liquidizer had given him. The taste was denser and more complex than that of the beef and onion, and it spread through his whole mouth. This alone would probably be enough to cover up any other memories, but the strange sensation in his chest still wouldn't quite go away.

Until now, Mikawa hadn't felt anything other than fear toward Liquidizer—at least, he didn't think so. He was grateful to her for rescuing him from the police and showing him how to live as a Ruby Eye, of course, but that was mutually beneficial. He was a useful asset to the Syndicate, after all. The only reason he was still going along with Liquidizer's demands was in order to make his dream of a Snowball Earth become a reality.

And yet.

In the fight at Minami-Aoyama, when Divider pointed a gun at Liquidizer, who'd been rendered unconscious by Accelerator's stun gun...

Despite knowing that he would die if he took another hit, he mustered the last of his strength to freeze Divider's gun. And when Divider asked why he didn't run away, his only answer was "I don't know."

Was it possible that something had changed for him since that moment?

Was that why his chest felt so strangely tight right now...?

"Boy...no, Mikawa."

Mikawa blinked, startled. It was strange to hear her call him by the name he'd chosen, even if it wasn't his real one.

Looking to his left, he saw that Liquidizer had finished eating her *okonomiyaki* and was looking at him with an unusually sincere expression.

"Wh…what is it?"

"To be honest, even if they use Empathizer's memory scan to seek out X, the member who killed those SDF members…I don't think they'll find anything."

"Huh…?"

Mikawa blinked again.

"You mean…a Ruby Eye that strong would be able to resist even Empathizer's power, you think?"

"Not quite. If someone resisted the scan, that would be as good as a confession, don't you agree? No, I have a feeling that X is an independent Ruby…one that doesn't belong to the Syndicate."

"No way… I mean…"

Mikawa furrowed his brow.

"It happened at a Syndicate hideout, didn't it? Why would an independent Ruby Eye be there?"

"Getting information about the hideout can't be any harder than killing six elite members of the Self-Defense Forces, as far as I'm concerned. Even the SFD members were able to find the safe house in Minami-Aoyama. Most likely, I'd imagine they tracked Empathizer's car with the N System. I told him not to use the boulevard…"

"…This is why that Peeping Tom can't be trusted."

"Well, we had to get rid of the car, so he'll be getting around on a moped for a while as punishment."

That sounded like a good punishment to Mikawa, although he himself usually traveled by foot or by train. He liked walking, but it did take much longer to get away from a crime scene that way, which was how Divider and an unidentified rifle user had followed him into Aoyama Park.

Maybe I should at least get a scooter or something, he thought as he replied.

"…If an independent Ruby who's not a Syndicate member really broke into the Keihinjima hideout and managed to kill a team of six Self-Defense Forces members…what on earth was the motive? Was he trying to show off his skills to get into the Syndicate or something?"

Liquidizer immediately shot down Mikawa's guess.

"I doubt it. If this person has such a strong attacking ability, we'd gladly accept them without a need for them to prove it in actual combat…assuming their personality and such suited us, of course. But in that case, surely this X person would contact the Syndicate, no? And since that hasn't happened, I think it served a different purpose."

"A different purpose…"

Mikawa repeated his former master's words, searching his brain for any other possibilities. Since he hadn't gone to school very much, he was a bit self-conscious at times that he might not be a sharp thinker, but if he decided to just give up thinking entirely, he wouldn't survive for long.

"…Could it be a coincidence that X fought with the SDF team? Maybe he'd been hiding out there for a while…in which case, his goal might be…"

Unconsciously, Mikawa gripped the wooden chopsticks in his right hand so hard that they creaked in protest. However, he didn't notice the noise and kept speaking in a low voice.

"Are they…trying to hunt not Jet Eyes but Ruby Eyes…? Syndicate members…?"

"*C'est bien.* I believe that is X's goal."

With that, Liquidizer picked up the last remaining piece of minced cucumber and snapped it neatly in half.

"……Well, unless……"

Mikawa thought he heard her murmur something else, but she didn't finish the thought out loud.

5

"Well, we're here. Thank you for everything today."

Minoru ducked his head once he got out of the car, and the Professor raised her right hand from the passenger's seat.

"Of course. Say hello to Oli-V for me."

"Yes, me too," Yumiko added from the driver's seat.

With that, she stepped on the accelerator pedal somewhat vigorously. When the red Alfa Romeo disappeared into the line of taillights streaming along Okubo Avenue, Minoru turned his face up.

The time was still before four o'clock, but the winter sky was already tinged with red. Since all the densely packed buildings in Tokyo limited the view of the sky, it got dark there more quickly than in Saitama.

The wind was colder than it had been in daytime, too, but strangely, Minoru didn't feel it. This might have been thanks to his Third Eye, but Minoru also thought he could still feel the warmth from having Suu Komura pressed against him.

"Thank goodness..."

A man who looked like an office worker glanced at Minoru when he mumbled to himself, but for once, Minoru didn't mind. If anything, all he felt was an urge to raise his fists in the air and shout for joy.

When Suu woke up from her coma, she promptly underwent a thorough examination, which confirmed that there were no serious complications that would affect her body or mind. Of course, she wouldn't be able to move around right away, so she would remain hospitalized in the ICU for a few days to be safe; but if she made good progress, she would apparently be transferred to a different hospital at the beginning of next week.

It was still unknown why Suu had woken up or what had happened inside the protective shell. Apparently, Suu herself barely even remembered sending the Morse code message with her finger. Dr. Hongou, who was knowledgeable about Third Eyes, wanted to inspect Minoru, too, but the Professor quickly stepped in on his behalf.

He was only able to talk with Suu Komura for five minutes after she woke up, so there was barely enough time to catch her up on the events of the last few days, and Minoru didn't get a chance to ask what he wanted to know most—the continuation of what she had said that day: *For the first time in my life, I...*

However, there was no need to rush. Once she was released from the ICU, Minoru would be able to go and visit her on his own.

The towering chalk-white building before Minoru's eyes now was the National Center of Advanced Health and Medicine (NCAM)—where Olivier Saito was currently admitted and the planned location of Suu Komura's transfer. The outside walls were more of a serene, sandy yellow than pure white, but the structure of the building, with the tallest part in the center and the other sections gradually getting lower on the left and right, called to mind a Western cathedral.

This hospital, the city's most prominent national health center, was the first in Japan to conduct an examination of Third Eyes—in other words, the place where Third Eyes were discovered. According to Yumiko, there was a rumor that the subject of the examination was Chief Himi himself and that he had bartered with the government to undergo this in exchange for approval of the founding of the SFD.

It was a strange story, but there was evidence to support it. NCAM's location was Shinjuku Ward, Toyama 1-chome—just over a quarter of a mile away in a straight line from the hidden location of SFD Headquarters in the park in Toyama 3-chome.

Currently, NCAM was at the forefront of Third Eye research and an important backup facility for the medical treatment of SFD members. There was a special area exclusively for Third Eye–related procedures on the eleventh floor, where the resident doctor had treated Minoru's seriously injured right hand three days ago and outfitted him with a high-tech cast.

Naturally, NCAM wasn't the only establishment that had a connection with the SFD. Within the twenty-three wards alone, there were apparently SFD-partnered hospitals in Hiroo, Tsukiji, Komagome, Yokohama, and even Saitama. The reason Suu was brought to Hiroo instead of NCAM was that the former was more specialized in cranial nerve damage, or so Minoru was told.

If it weren't for Chief Himi, there probably wouldn't be such an accommodating health care system in place. In fact, the SFD might not exist at all.

On the other hand, the Ruby Eyes who fought against the SFD probably couldn't hope to attain such advanced medical backup, no matter how organized they might be. How did they treat their own injuries?

What had happened to the seriously injured Liquidizer and Trancer after they liquefied the ground and fled three days ago?

With these thoughts on the back of his mind, Minoru took his smartphone out from his jacket's inner pocket, checking the time. When he contacted Olivier Saito to say he wanted to pay him a visit, the response was "anytime after four," but that was still almost ten minutes away.

Figuring he could walk slowly and listen to music, Minoru pushed his phone's earbuds into his ears. Setting the playback on shuffle, he crossed Ooku Avenue and entered the hospital grounds.

Since it was January 3, still part of the national New Year's holiday, the front entrance was closed. Instead, Minoru went around to the side entrance on the left of the building and entered using the key card they'd made for him when his right hand was being treated.

The lights were down in the wide entrance hall, and there was no sign of anyone around. He peeked through the nearby after-hours reception window, but there was no one there, either.

Wondering if even the hospital suspended work entirely for the New Year's holiday, Minoru headed farther inside toward the elevator. At the very least, the 3E Committee should still have a guard stationed on the eleventh floor, and of course, Olivier Saito would be in his room.

Minoru used the controls on the earphone cord to lower the volume of the music as he walked through the dimly lit hallway. Then, when he had made it about five meters down the hall, it happened.

Suddenly, Minoru smelled a faint odor.

Mixed in with the antiseptic smell of the hospital was something altogether different. A raw, metallic, beastly smell...

The smell of a Ruby Eye.

"......!!"

A powerful shudder ran up his back, and the middle of his chest throbbed. It was the Third Eye's passive reaction to the threat that Minoru hadn't yet perceived. Reflexively gulping down air, Minoru tried to activate his protective shell.

However, he was a second too late.

A sharp pain toward the right side of the back of his neck made Minoru gasp. The air expelled from his lungs, preventing him from pressing the "switch" in his chest.

Staggering and dropping his left knee to the floor, Minoru touched his right hand to the nape of his neck. It felt a little sticky. Blood. He'd been stabbed by something.

Judging by the amount of blood, though, it wasn't a deep wound. His major blood vessels seemed safe. The damage was negligible—he could ignore it for now. What he needed to do was locate the enemy...

But this thought was blown away by a second rush of intense pain.

"Agh...!"

Minoru gasped out a little cry of pain, curling his body inward. The wound on his neck... No, it felt as if something inside it was being bored into by a sharp blade.

Minoru instinctively felt out the identity of the pain.

Some tiny thing was moving just under his skin. It was tearing through his muscles, burrowing in somewhere even deeper. Almost like a parasite.

This was an attack by a Ruby Eye.

If the source of the pain reached his blood vessels—the common carotid artery—it would all be over.

That thought brought with it a flood of panic, but Minoru quashed it as best he could. The common carotid artery was about two centimeters below the skin. He had at least ten seconds before that thing would reach it. Whether he lived or died would depend on the next handful of moments.

There was no doubt that the foreign object digging into his neck was the ability of a Ruby Eye hiding somewhere nearby. Most likely, the Ruby Eye was controlling this object from a distance. In which case, if he could interrupt the so-called seventh-force link between the Ruby Eye and the parasite-like object, the latter should stop moving.

There was only one way to do this. He had to move his mouth and throat, which were stiffened with pain, so that he could breathe in air and activate his shell.

Forcing his involuntarily clenched teeth to pry open, fighting to expand his blocked-up respiratory tract, Minoru managed to squeeze a little bit of air into his lungs.

It wasn't nearly as much as he normally used to activate the sensory switch of the Third Eye. But right now, it was the most he could do.

Connect!!

For some reason, this was the word that Minoru thought with all his might, not *defend* or *close*, as he pressed the Third Eye's switch.

His body floated upward, and the color of the floor changed.

The pain in his neck eased little by little, gradually subsiding into a dull ache.

The foreign object was still inside him, but it seemed to have stopped moving. However, it was probably close to his artery by now. If he moved his neck too far, it might break through a blood vessel.

It was at this point that Minoru finally noticed that music was still playing in his ears. Gently, he tugged the earbuds out with his left hand, hanging them over his shoulder.

Now all that was left in this silent world was the mysterious low rhythm. That and the violent pounding of Minoru's heart. On top of that, he could hear his own shallow, rapid breathing.

As long as he kept still, the foreign object shouldn't scratch his artery. However, because of the holiday, the first floor of the hospital was completely empty. It was unlikely that anyone would come through here, and if an ordinary civilian were to enter, the hidden Ruby Eye might attack them.

…No, wait.

Even on a holiday, wasn't it unnatural for the reception desk to be unmanned? And Minoru had entered the building with a key card. It was highly possible that any staff members who might have been at the reception desk had already been attacked by the Ruby Eye.

He couldn't stay at a standstill much longer. He had to neutralize the enemy before anyone else got hurt.

Shifting from one knee to all fours, Minoru let the strength out of his left arm, then his right leg, collapsing on the spot. He closed his eyes, letting his entire body go limp.

He was playing dead, or rather, playing unconscious. The enemy probably knew as well as he did that the Third Eye exodus would occur if its host died, so he wouldn't be able to pass for dead. Instead, pretending to have passed out was more likely to fool the enemy—provided they didn't notice that Minoru's body was floating slightly above the floor. It was a chance he would have to take.

The problem was that Minoru couldn't hear any sounds outside his shell, so he had no way of knowing the enemy's movements with his eyes closed. *I'll have to ask the Professor to find a way around this problem soon...* But Minoru quickly banished this idle thought, focusing all his efforts on pretending to be unconscious.

All he could count on now was his intuition—his sixth sense. It wasn't exactly scientific, but if the Third Eye's seventh force existed, then surely the sixth sense did as well.

Forcing himself to resist the urge to crack his eyes open, Minoru waited.

Try to imagine what the enemy is thinking. If I were the type of person to ambush others, I would still be trying to gauge the situation. I'd observe for a good two...no, three minutes...making sure the enemy was really unconscious before I move. So not yet...not quite yet. A little longer...just a little bit longer, and......

Minoru thought he felt the hair on the nape of his neck move.

Instantly, he opened his eyes.

Then he saw it. Just three meters away, there was a person crouching down to peer at Minoru's face.

The person was tall and thin, but Minoru couldn't tell whether they were male or female, young or old. They were wearing a dark-red coat that looked like rubber, with the hood pulled down over their face, and since there was an entrance directly behind them, their face was completely dark.

But one thing was clear: This was no ordinary passerby looking at the fallen Minoru with concern. It was, without a doubt, the mystery Ruby Eye who had assaulted him.

Because in the unknown person's outstretched right hand was a large needle. No well-intentioned individual would suddenly try to inject something into an unconscious person. That syringe was a symbol of malice.

The enemy seemed startled that Minoru's eyes had opened, and they stood up with a snap.

Taking care to move his neck as little as possible, Minoru pushed against the floor with all his strength and stood up.

If the enemy's ability was to remotely manipulate a small but deadly weapon, then Minoru was in no danger of taking further damage as long as his shell was protecting him. And since the person wasn't very large, a punch from Minoru's shield-enforced fist should be enough to knock them out.

As Minoru charged forward, the enemy's left hand moved toward him.

There was something strange attached to the palm of the hand, which was covered by a dark-red glove the same color as the coat.

It was a metal disc, no more than two centimeters in diameter. There was a small hole in the slightly raised center. It was almost like a nozzle.

As if to confirm Minoru's intuition, something fired out of the hole. It was a very thin thread of some kind, around fifty centimeters in length.

It doesn't matter what it is!

Minoru tried to ignore the thread and throw a punch.

But suddenly, his legs wouldn't move, as if they were caught in something.

"......?!"

Minoru tumbled helplessly to the floor. Thanks to the shell, he didn't take any damage, but the wound in his neck throbbed painfully.

Ignoring it, Minoru looked at his legs. Then he widened his eyes.

Outside the shell, some kind of thin wire was wrapped around his ankles, obstructing his movement. The wire only looked to be about three millimeters thick. It seemed like it would be easy to tear, but no matter how hard he tried, even Minoru's Third Eye–enhanced strength couldn't budge it.

The enemy had backed away considerably, with one foot through the door of the entrance, but they stopped there in a strange posture to look down at Minoru. Most likely, they were trying to decide whether to run away or attack again. Minoru still couldn't see their face beneath the hood.

At present, Minoru's protective shell's greatest weakness was that he couldn't move if he was tightly restrained from outside of it. When he was buried in concrete by Liquidizer's power or closed in liquefied iron, he physically hadn't been able to do a thing.

There was a way to remove the constraints, though: the new "burst" power he'd come up with in order to escape from the concrete. He could diffuse the protective shell explosively, blowing away whatever was restraining him.

However, once he did this, he couldn't make another shell for about three minutes. On top of that, the enemy's deadly device was still embedded in Minoru's neck. If he started to move again, his carotid artery would be ruptured in a matter of seconds. So, just as he thought, he wouldn't be able to use "burst" right now.

"Ngh...nnngh!"

Groaning, Minoru put all his strength into trying to tear off the wire.

Since the protective shell was impenetrably hard, he could do this without worrying about hurting himself. At this level of thinness, he was sure he could break even stainless steel wire. However, though the mysterious substance the enemy had launched from their palm seemed somewhat elastic, it gave no sign of breaking.

Seeing that Minoru couldn't move, the enemy slowly stepped forward again.

As they approached with caution, they raised the syringe in their right hand.

There was no need to fear that the syringe would penetrate his shell, but Minoru stared at it anyway, wondering what his mysterious opponent was trying to inject into him.

"......!!"

Then he noticed it. The piston of the syringe was fully pushed in. There was nothing inside.

So that syringe was...

At that moment, the enemy quickly looked up. Reflexively, Minoru also turned to look.

Behind them, about eighteen meters away, one of the elevators that lined the wall was starting to open. Someone had come down.

Oh no—they'll be killed...

Minoru clenched his teeth. If the enemy tried to kill an innocent person, he had to stop that no matter what, even if he had to use "burst."

Lowering the syringe, the enemy raised their left hand instead. The nozzle in the center of the palm glinted faintly in the backlight.

Even knowing that no one could hear him, Minoru started to shout "Get away!" but he swallowed his words partway through.

The person who leaped out of the elevator was wearing nothing but white bandages that covered his chest and pajama pants—and holding an unsheathed Japanese sword in his right hand.

Minoru didn't even need to see the loose, wavy hair and the handsome, foreign-looking face to know that it was the member of the SFD with the code name Divider: Olivier Saito. He had probably smelled the Ruby Eye from the eleventh floor.

As Olivier took in the situation with a glance and dashed forward fiercely, the Ruby Eye launched something toward him from the palm of their left hand.

It wasn't the wire that was binding Minoru's legs. It was much smaller, like a thorn only two to five centimeters long. Even with his enhanced kinetic vision, Minoru could barely follow it with his eyes, but he still realized that it must be the same weapon that was lodged in his own neck.

"Don't let it hit you!" Minoru yelled, then realized Olivier couldn't hear him inside the shell.

He started to deactivate it, accepting the risk that the object in his neck might move again, but then—

The sword that had been hanging loosely from Olivier's hand swung up from the bottom and swept to the right at a terrifying speed. Sparks burst from the edge of the blade, and immediately, a yellow light flashed on the side of the thick pillar behind Olivier to his left. Minoru couldn't hear the sound, but it looked as though the small object had been repelled by the sword, collided with the pillar, and exploded.

The explosion was miniscule, no more intense than a firecracker, but it would undoubtedly be no small matter if it happened inside a person's body. An explosion like that near a major organ or a thick blood vessel, like the common carotid artery, would surely kill any victim, Third Eye or no.

Minoru was intensely aware of the foreign object still embedded in his neck, but he forced the fear down, kicking off the floor with his still-restrained legs. The friction coefficient of the shell's surface was normally near zero but could be focused on a specific point of contact if he was moving or grabbing something. Taking advantage of this unique characteristic, Minoru glided across the ceramic tile floor as if skating on ice.

Aiming at the legs of the Ruby Eye who was trying to fire another shot from the nozzle, Minoru slammed into the person's legs, shell and all.

Apparently, the enemy had been focusing on Olivier—their reaction was a moment too late to stop Minoru from knocking them off-balance. Once the Ruby Eye was on the floor, Minoru planned to cover them with his body, giving Olivier time to close the eighteen-meter distance between them. Judging that the foreign object in his neck wouldn't touch the carotid artery so long as he didn't move too much, Minoru reached both hands toward his opponent, planning to simply weigh the person down instead of engaging in hand-to-hand combat.

But in that instant—

Just as the enemy was about to hit the floor, they aimed their left palm away from Olivier and toward the entrance.

This time, it was extremely thin wire that fired from the nozzle.

The wire that hit the wall near the entrance was several times longer than the one around Minoru's legs.

Immediately, the body of the enemy switched from falling to speeding away to the side.

The wire, secured to the wall, was pulling the enemy's body like a winch. The hem of the red coat beat through the air until the Ruby Eye landed in front of the entrance. The wire flew back to their left hand as they opened the door with their right and fled outside.

A few seconds later, Olivier reached Minoru. He already seemed to have seen what was stopping Minoru from rising, and with a swing of his sword, he cut through the incredibly strong wire in an instant. But Olivier's body was shaking as he turned to follow the enemy through the door.

"O...Oli-V!"

Calling from inside the shell, Minoru stood up.

Just as Olivier collapsed to his left, Minoru caught him through the shell. Looking closer, he saw that the bandages that covered his chest, abdomen, and both shoulders were dyed a vivid red in several places. ·

The wounds from three days ago, when he took a direct hit from the Ruby Eye Trancer's ice bomb, had opened up again because of his vigorous movements.

Olivier grimaced in pain for a few seconds in the arms of the alarmed Minoru, but then he quickly braced himself and stood up. At first, he started to head toward the entrance again, but then he stopped, probably realizing that he wouldn't be able to catch up with the Ruby Eye now.

Perhaps because he was still hospitalized, Olivier wasn't wearing his usual blue glasses as he turned to look at Minoru. Even in this situation, and despite the fact that they were the same gender, Minoru couldn't help but be captivated by the frustrated Olivier's good looks for a moment. Then he noticed that the other boy was saying something, but he couldn't hear it through the protective shell.

"Um...there's some kind of remote-controlled needle in here, so I can't deactivate the shell."

Pointing at his neck with his cast-bound right hand, Minoru moved his arm exaggeratedly as he spoke. Furrowing his brow, Olivier put his left hand on Minoru's right shoulder over the shell and peered at his neck. His expression turned grave at once, and he nodded, taking a small smartphone out of the pocket of his pajama pants.

After a short call, Olivier ran a slim finger across the screen, then turned it toward Minoru. There was a message displayed on the screen: "The Professor is coming. Sit down for now."

Minoru started to nod, then widened his eyes.

He'd assumed the Ruby Eye had escaped, but what if that had been a feint and the attacker was still hiding nearby? They might even try to attack the Professor with a needle when she arrived. Without any way to interrupt the remote-control connection, she wouldn't be able to remove the needle quickly enough.

"It's too dangerous; the enemy could still be nearby..."

Olivier seemed to understand the movements of Minoru's lips this time. Again, he nodded and flicked the smartphone screen.

"Apparently, DD just got back, so he's coming, too. If there's a Ruby nearby, he'll notice for sure."

Even Minoru couldn't argue with that statement.

Denjirou Daimon, also known as Searcher, didn't have any offensive abilities, but in exchange his detection abilities were extremely long-ranged. Minoru and the others could tell if a Ruby Eye was using their powers nearby, in the form of a beastly smell, but DD could sense them in a ninety-meter radius even if they didn't use their abilities.

So if DD was with her, there was no chance of a surprise attack... Logically, Minoru understood this, but he still felt uneasy.

This Ruby Eye could fire small needles or elastic wire from the palm of their hand and manipulate them at will.

There was no telling how the mechanism worked, but it could be classified as a relatively simple Third Eye ability. It wasn't quite so terrifying as Liquidizer's ability to liquefy anything or Igniter's ability to manipulate oxygen.

But there was something about that which made the red-coated Ruby Eye all the more sinister. This ability was quiet and inconspicuous, like an assassin.

Minoru wanted to go outside and keep watch until Professor Riri Isa and company arrived, but he forced himself to sit in a chair in the lobby and wait with Olivier, which only took about five minutes.

The red Alfa Romeo pulled up in the rotary in front of the hospital, white smoke billowing from its tires as it slid to a stop, upon which Yumiko Azu burst out of the driver's seat.

Initially, she charged at the automatic door, then made a face quite unbecoming of a high school girl when she realized it wouldn't open and used her ability to dash away to the right. Within ten seconds, the side entrance opened, and Yumiko reappeared.

Next, she used her acceleration ability to close the eighteen-meter distance in an instant, skidding to a halt in front of Minoru. Grabbing his shoulders over the shell with both hands, she shouted something inaudible.

Having somewhat expected this turn of events, Minoru awkwardly operated the smartphone grasped in his left hand inside the shell, holding it up to show a two-word memo to Yumiko: "i'm fine."

Yumiko, who was apparently quite a worrywart despite her usual tart attitude, relaxed her sharp features into an expression of earnest relief and finally let go of his shoulders. Then she turned to Olivier, who was sitting at Minoru's right, and commenced a rapid conversation.

The door opened again, and the Professor and DD came inside. Olivier must have told them to exercise extreme caution, as DD was gripping an automatic pistol in his right hand and staring around wildly beneath the brim of his trademark cap.

At this point, Minoru finally considered how strange it was that no security guards had come onto the scene in spite of all the commotion. It was possible that Olivier had told the 3E Committee guard stationed on the eleventh floor not to come down, but there was probably a security guardroom on this floor, too. Trying to look around without moving his neck, Minoru noticed a window next to the reception desk that seemed to fit the bill. But it was completely dark inside, with no sign of any people.

Minoru sat preoccupied with anxious premonitions as the Professor jogged up to him and showed him the screen of her phone: "explain the situation, please."

Minoru nodded and typed up a rather long text on his own smartphone.

The small foreign object that was still in the right side of his neck, too close to a major artery for comfort. The possibility that it might start moving again if he deactivated the shell. And the fact that it might explode if it were attacked...

Reading his message, the Professor nodded grimly and contacted someone on her phone.

A few minutes later, two of the elevators opened at almost the exact same time, and two men wearing white coats, one guard in a black uniform, and two stretchers appeared. Prompted by a brisk hand wave, Minoru lay down on the stretcher, and Yumiko, not the staff in white coats, began to push it. The exasperated expression of the Professor vanished in an instant, and Minoru was brought back to the 3E area where his right hand had been treated just three days ago.

One hour later—5:20 p.m.

For the first time in some while, five SFD members gathered in a meeting space on the fifth floor of headquarters.

Professor Riri Isa, Yumiko Azu, DD, Minoru, and Olivier Saito. Unfortunately, Suu Komura wasn't physically present, but the meeting was being relayed to her hospital room via webcam.

The Professor had tried to tell Olivier to stay in the hospital, since his wounds had just reopened, but he managed to get permission to leave temporarily after insisting that he'd go back immediately after.

The reason he didn't give in was simple: The bodies of one hospital staff member and one security guard had been found inside the after-hours reception desk and the security guardroom.

Sitting in a chair with the help of DD, Olivier's face was twisted with regret as he spoke.

"Damn it, why didn't I notice...? If that damn red-coat bastard was using their abilities in the same building as me, I should've smelled it right away."

The Professor shook her head gently at Olivier, who had thrown on a fleece parka over his pajamas.

"We checked the images from the security cameras, and found that those two were attacked at ten a.m. this morning. You were sleeping under an analgesic at the time, remember? There was no way you could've noticed."

"...That stupid sadistic doctor said I'd heal faster if I slept..."

Olivier muttered darkly, and the Professor gave a faint, bitter smile.

The sadistic doctor in question was Dr. Satoru Nitamizu, who single-handedly managed the NCAM's Third Eye research. Apparently, the man, a leading expert on neurophysiology, was also a friend of Chief Himi's from his student days, but if Chief Himi had the air of a military man, then Dr. Nitamizu had that of an aristocrat. He had an intimidatingly elegant demeanor and refined manner of speaking, but he was also the person who made the high-tech cast on Minoru's right hand and who had just removed the foreign object from Minoru's neck with expert speed and precision.

Minoru gently touched a hand to the protective patch affixed to his neck.

"I think that's true, though. According to Dr. Nitamizu's analysis, when we sleep, our Third Eyes shift their focus from strengthening to healing and stuff..."

"Hmm, be careful there, Mikkun. If that man takes a liking to you, no good can come of it."

"I—I don't think he's particularly taken a liking to me or anything..."

This time, it was Yumiko who chimed in with a serious expression.

"If you ask me, the way that old man looks at you is awfully suspicious."

"Y-Yumiko, you too...?"

"Those eyes are saying he wants to dissect you someday, Utsugi. Don't go with him if he invites you out to dinner or anything, all right?"

"......"

Minoru fell silent for a moment, remembering that Dr. Nitamizu once said, *I'll treat you to something to celebrate once your wounds heal,* but he decided to forget about that for the time being and focused on the Professor, who was now standing at the front of the room.

"So, Professor...what was the cause of death of the two people who passed away?"

"Hmm... Yes, let's start from there, shall we?"

The Professor cleared her throat and moved her fingers across the tablet in her hand. A somewhat grainy image appeared on the two-meter monitor behind her. It showed a corner of a confined room, where a female staff member wearing a cardigan over her vest-style uniform and a male guard in a navy-blue security uniform were slumped in a heap.

"The hospital staffer is Ms. Miya Yoshijima, and the security guard is Mr. Takanori Sakai. At 10:07 this morning, Mr. Sakai finished his outside patrol and was opening the side entrance when the culprit—the red-coated Ruby Eye who fought against Mikkun—killed him with a long-distance attack. As far as we can tell from the security camera image, it was a nearly instantaneous death. When Mr. Sakai fell, the culprit entered the building before the door closed and dragged the body inside. The culprit's reason for targeting the NCAM is still unknown."

"W...wait a minute."

The voice belonged to DD, who had thus far been silent (since he was busy eating a meat bun he'd apparently bought at a convenience store).

"You said the guard was killed instantly from a distance as soon as he started to enter the building, right? Without a gun, what Ruby Eye ability could possibly kill someone instantly at such a precise moment?"

That doubt was quite natural.

All Third Eye abilities—not just Ruby Eyes'—were based around manipulating specific molecules. The variety of molecules one could manipulate generally decreased in proportion to the range of the user.

For instance, the Biter, the first Ruby Eye that Minoru fought, had the power to strengthen his mouth and teeth. The molecules he manipulated ranged from protein to metal, but that was because as a transformation-type ability user, the range of its use was almost zero.

On the other hand, users like Igniter and Trancer who had a range of several meters could only manipulate very limited kinds of molecules, like oxygen or hydrogen. They were still powerful enough, but it was unlikely that they would be able to kill someone instantly from such a distance.

"Hmm... Well, have a look at this."

The Professor ran a finger over the tablet, and the image on the monitor changed.

What was displayed now was the side entrance of NCAM, which Minoru had passed through just an hour ago. This must be the security camera image the Professor had mentioned.

Right away, a uniformed security guard entered the frame from the right side of the screen. Stopping in front of the door, he pressed the key card to the sensor with a practiced movement. Just after he pushed the door open with his right hand and took a step inside, the security guard froze. Tilting his head, he pressed his left hand to his left ear—then his body stiffened, and he fell to the ground.

"...That was only three seconds after he opened the door...," Yumiko murmured in a hoarse voice, and Minoru gulped.

Slumped on the threshold of the entrance, the security guard's body prevented the door from closing. Immediately afterward, a red silhouette appeared. It was the hooded Ruby Eye.

"Bastard...," Olivier croaked in a low voice.

The murderer had a slender figure but still displayed the brute strength of a Ruby Eye, pulling the security guard inside with just one hand. The figures disappeared, the door closed without a sound, and the video ended.

"...After this, the culprit used the same method to kill Ms. Yoshijima, who was at the after-hours reception desk, and hid the two bodies inside the reception area. Unfortunately, this was in the camera's blind spot, but the criminal was most likely hiding in the same place."

Without thinking, Minoru tilted his head at this explanation. The scar on the right side of his neck throbbed, so he hurriedly straightened up while he spoke.

"Um...this video took place shortly after ten a.m., right? And it was four in the evening when I went to visit Oli-V... So the criminal was hidden behind the reception window for six hours, but nobody found them?"

"So it would seem."

The Professor pulled up the floor plan for the first floor of the hospital on the monitor.

"The hospital was closed until today for the New Year, and visitation for patients was limited to emergencies. On top of that, the emergency outpatient area at NCAM is in a different building, and the entrance is quite far away. In other words, the first floor of this central building was nearly empty. Still, staff members did pass through the side entrance several times in the course of the six hours, but none of them seemed to notice that nobody was at the reception window. If they had noticed and looked inside, they probably would've been killed as well..."

"...So this Ruby Eye is the type that doesn't choose targets, like Trancer, then."

"I guess so," Olivier spat in agreement with DD.

Minoru understood what he meant by "choosing targets," too.

There were two predominant types of Ruby Eyes: those who carefully chose the targets of their killings and those who were only concerned with the method of the murder.

Biter was one representative of the former type. Masquerading as the gourmet critic Hikaru Takaesu, he patterned himself after a shark and chose the victims he bit to death according to his aesthetic sense. He had attempted to kill Minoru's friend Tomomi Minowa because she was healthy and athletic, with strong bones.

On the other hand, there were Ruby Eyes like Trancer, who had caused a large-scale accident that killed seven people just six days ago: He preferred to commit his murders on rainy or snowy days but didn't care who he killed. What DD was saying was that this "red coat" Ruby Eye was likely the same way.

This made sense to Minoru, but in the back of his mind, something still weighed on him. Just as he was about to put his finger on the reason, the Professor spoke again.

"It's true that this Ruby Eye doesn't seem to choose targets, but it's possible that our culprit doesn't care about the means, either."

"What do you mean? It certainly seems as though they do all their killing with their ability to me..."

Without answering Yumiko out loud, the Professor operated the tablet again.

The monitor changed to yet another image, this time displaying a large, unfamiliar object.

"...An insect...?" Yumiko murmured, puzzled.

Minoru had the same first impression.

The strange item on the screen had an elongated teardrop shape. The sharp, pointed end had a glossy black luster, while the larger end was dark red. There was a spiral groove carved around from the point to the middle of the object, and the large end had sparse hairlike growths. If it wasn't an insect, it looked like it might be some kind of seed.

"Ew... I wouldn't wanna get anywhere near those things. What are they anyway?"

Finishing his meat bun, DD balled up the paper bag as he spoke, and the Professor gave a sidelong glance at Minoru before answering.

"This is what was removed from Mikkun's neck."

"Geh!" Olivier yelped on Minoru's right, and "Whoa!" shouted DD from two chairs to the left. At the same time, both of them scooched several centimeters away from Minoru, chairs and all.

However, Yumiko, in the seat at his immediate left, stayed composed and scolded the two boys.

"Don't react like elementary school children, you two. It's already been removed from Utsugi, remember?"

At this, DD and Olivier sheepishly returned their seats to normal, and Minoru managed to resist the urge to scratch his neck. On the other hand, though, he couldn't resist the urge to test whether Yumiko's unperturbed state was the real thing...

"Ah, Yumiko, on your shoulder!"

With this exclamation, Minoru reached out as if to pluck some small object from her shoulder with his left hand.

"YAAAAAAH!"

With a tremendous shriek, the Accelerator literally jumped out of her chair. The recoil from her kicking off the floor was clearly stronger than she anticipated, as she went up a couple of meters in the air before landing back in her seat with an audible *thump*. And her panic didn't subside there.

"Where, where?!"

Now I've done it, Minoru thought as Yumiko frantically brushed her right shoulder with her hand.

"U-um... I'm sorry, it was a joke..."

"...What? Wait. Whaaaaat?"

Raising an increasingly shrill cry, Yumiko's right hand shot out at superhuman speed and pinched Minoru's cheek between her thumb and index finger. Restraining her Jet Eye strength, she nevertheless put a great deal of power into her fingers as she yanked his cheek painfully, eliciting a helpless shout from Minoru.

"Owowowowww!"

"Listen up! Next time you pull a prank on me, I'll do this three times as hard, got it?!"

"I-I-I'm sorryyy!"

Minoru apologized for dear life, but Yumiko showed no signs of letting go.

As he tried to continue repeating his apology despite the tears welling up in his eyes, Minoru suddenly thought he heard someone laughing. DD and Olivier looked frightened, and the Professor seemed rather cross, so it wasn't any of them. The source of the giggling voice seemed to be the speakers of the laptop computer on the desk nearby.

A moment later, Yumiko noticed the laughter, too, and finally released Minoru's cheek. Olivier and the others looked at the PC, too, and the laughter gradually subsided, until eventually a girl's husky voice came through the speakers.

"...Sorry, I shouldn't have laughed. It's just, it was just so funny."

This was unmistakably the voice of the Refractor, Suu Komura. Finally remembering that the video of the meeting was being relayed to Suu's hospital room, he turned toward the PC in a panic.

"N-no, I'm the one who should be sorry for joking around at a time like this..."

"No need to apologize to me. The SFD has always been like this."

Yumiko shrugged in response to Suu's words.

"Yes, I suppose that's true. It's mostly DD's fault, though."

"Huh? Why me?! No way, I'm the most serious guy in the whole shebang!"

DD continued protesting until Olivier cut in.

"No, I agree, it is D&D's fault. I mean, you were eating a meat bun during half the meeting."

"Wh-what's wrong with that? I took the Kanetsu nonstop train back here, so I didn't get to eat lunch. Besides, if you want the organization to get serious, maybe you should quit calling me D&D for starters, Oli!"

"Really? Okay, then we'll call you Advanced Denjirou Daimon, or for short..."

"Stop, that's even worse!"

The back-and-forth volley between the two made Suu collapse into giggles again.

"Oh, how nice... I hope I can come back soon, too."

At that, Olivier quit grinning long enough to respond so loudly it seemed like he was trying to make his voice reach the hospital in Hiroo.

"Yeah, come back soon, Hinacchi! We'll throw you the best welcome-back party ever!"

Having recovered from their physical disgust at the mysterious insect thanks to the unplanned comedy act, the group focused on the monitor again.

Taking out a laser pointer, Professor Riri Isa resumed her commentary.

"They've only just started dissecting it in NCAM, but this pointy little thing... Dr. Nitamizu has taken to calling it a 'spinebug,' so we'll go with that for now... It appears to be some kind of pseudo-living creature created by the ability of the unknown Ruby Eye who attacked the hospital. It's incredibly small, only seven millimeters long and three millimeters wide at the widest point. But being stabbed with it would probably hurt much more than a needle...is that correct, Mikkun?"

Minoru winced, remembering the pain from when the spinebug stabbed his neck.

"Yeah...it was more like an awl drilling into me or something."

"*Drilling* is probably an apt word for it. Everyone, please look at the thorn section closely."

The laser pointer's light drew a circle around the sharp, pointed end.

"This thorn has a helix-shaped spiral carved around it, just like a drill. Apparently, it's made of iron nitride."

"And what is iron nitride...?"

The Professor answered Yumiko's question smoothly, without consulting anything.

"As the name suggests, it's iron fused with nitrogen. There are several different variations on the molecular structure, but Fe_2N, which this drill is made of, is often used for surface treatment of mechanical parts. However, the rear part of the bug—the swollen portion and the hairs that grow from it—they're made up of an unknown protein, not metal. The structure of the hair is very similar to that of the flagella possessed by some microorganisms."

"Flagella... Does that mean these things move?"

The Professor nodded at Olivier's question.

"Mm-hmm. This is just speculation, but we believe that when this spinebug pierces human skin, it uses its flagella to rotate itself and burrow deeper like a drill. There was a two-centimeter scar in Mikkun's neck where the spinebug broke through his muscle. If it had gone three millimeters farther, it would've reached the common carotid artery."

Although he'd more or less known that at the time, hearing it put into words brought Minoru back to the terror of that moment. Unconsciously, he touched the protective patch with his fingers again.

With a glance at Minoru, Yumiko spoke from his left side.

"But even if it did, that wouldn't be the end, would it? No matter how important the blood vessel, I can't imagine a hole of only a few millimeters could kill someone instantly like that."

"You're right. Judging by the images on the security camera, the spinebugs' goal isn't to damage the blood vessels or organs with drilling."

"What happens after the bug enters the carotid artery?"

Minoru had already guessed the answer. The moment when Olivier deflected the projectile fired from the red-coated Ruby Eye's left hand had given him a frightening clue. After that, the bug that hit the pillar of the wall had...

"They explode...right?"

All eyes in the room turned toward Minoru. Usually, this sort of scene would make him wither immediately, but he seemed to have built up some resistance, or else the conversation before had affected him, because now he was able to continue speaking without hesitation.

"I'm only guessing, but the swelled part at the back of the bug... couldn't there be some kind of explosive substance in there? I mean, when Oli-V blocked one of the bugs earlier..."

Minoru pointedly turned toward Olivier, whose eyes blinked for a moment behind his blue-framed glasses before widening in realization.

"Ooh...so that was a spinebug? I thought it was some kind of firecracker or something... So that means, if I hadn't blocked that thing, one of those insects would've gone into my body and..."

Olivier shuddered, and Minoru nodded gravely.

"That's exactly right... Well, the explosion I saw was really only about as intense as a firecracker, but if that were inside your body—especially near your heart or your brain—I think that'd be a fatal wound even for a Jet Eye."

"Most likely. In fact, that's exactly how Ms. Yoshijima and Mr. Sakai were killed. The spinebug entered through the ear, pierced the eardrum, and exploded inside the cochlea, fatally injuring the brain."

After the Professor spoke, DD's voice was thick with thinly veiled anger and fear.

"...So that's why the security guard put a hand on his ear in the security video..."

"Mm-hmm. It's likely that our red coat's standard tactic is to send a spinebug through the ear to destroy the brain."

Imagining an insect drilling into his ear, Minoru ducked his head, his ear canal feeling itchy. His freshly treated wound throbbed painfully, which brought yet another question to mind.

"Wait, but...why did the spinebug enter my neck, not my ear, then...?"

But even as he voiced the question, Minoru realized the answer himself.

"...Oh, wait... I...I was wearing earbuds."

"Exactly. You got lucky, Mikkun."

The Professor snapped her fingers and pointed at Minoru's right ear.

"If you weren't wearing the earbuds, the spinebug most likely would've entered your ear. In that case, you still could have prevented the explosion by activating your shell, but there's a nonzero possibility that you wouldn't have made it in time."

"More than 'nonzero'... I'm pretty sure I wouldn't have made it. If I didn't know what was going on, I probably would've just assumed a fly had buzzed into my ear or something. It would've startled me, but I doubt I would've put up my protective shell because of it."

Sitting on his left and listening, Yumiko stared intently at the spinebug on the screen.

"But...it can only carry the amount of explosives that would fit into its body, right? That's got to be ten or twenty milligrams at most... Would that really make a big enough explosion to destroy the brain?"

"Excellent question. Take a look at this."

The Professor touched the tablet again, advancing the slide on the screen.

This picture showed the NCAM hall where the fight against the red coat had taken place just an hour ago. In the next photo, it focused on one of the four rectangular pillars. There was a distinct burn mark on the surface in a radial shape.

"...The residue left behind by the explosion here has just been ana-lyzed. The substance is called acetone peroxide."

"What...?!" Yumiko exclaimed in surprise.

"Acetone peroxide is what they call TATP, isn't it? It's a high-performance explosive often used by terrorists... In which case, even a tiny amount would certainly pack enough power to kill someone, but how could that stuff be inside such a tiny pseudo-creature? Does that mean...the insects were made with the ability, then manually filled with TATP?"

"No, that's highly doubtful."

The Professor shook her head, then looked at Minoru.

"According to Mikkun's explanation, the Ruby Eye—let's call them Red Coat—shot the spinebugs from their left palm, right?"

"Right..."

Minoru nodded and tried to explain the strange object that had been attached to Red Coat's palm.

"The Ruby Eye was wearing gloves, but in the middle of the left one, there was something that looked like a smooth metal nozzle attached... The insects shot out of that. I think maybe the materials were stored in the gloves, and that fired at the same time as the insects were made. It definitely didn't seem like they were manually stuffing explosives into every single bug."

"Hmm..."

The Professor nodded shortly, then folded her arms. Her white lab coat fluttered as she paced back and forth in front of the screen.

"...The constituent elements of the spinebug are iron nitrate for the drill portion and protein for the body... So carbon, hydrogen, oxygen, nitro-gen, and phosphorus. They're all common chemical elements, so they'd be easy to obtain, and they could probably be put into a plastic bag or something and hidden inside a glove... No, wait. The chemical formula of TATP is $C_9H_{18}O_6$, so that's still only carbon, hydrogen, and oxygen. So it could easily be generated from the same materials as the bug..."

As the Professor muttered to herself rapidly, DD raised his hand con-scientiously for permission to speak.

"Um, 'scuse me, Professor..."

"Go ahead, DD."

"So this Red Coat fella's ability is to, uh...make little murder bugs full of explosives out of iron, nitrogen, protein, and stuff, right? But Mikkun said the Ruby was controlling the bugs after they were made and fired, didn't he?"

Feeling eyes on him, Minoru nodded firmly.

"Yeah. It definitely felt like the spinebug in my neck was moving according to the Ruby Eye's will. And it stopped moving once I activated my shell... If it was really perfectly autonomous, it would've kept moving."

"Hmm, no objections so far. And?"

Urged on by the Professor, DD gestured vigorously as he spoke.

"So, uh...that means that Red Coat can control bugs made of at least six different elements from a distance. But doesn't that go against the rule that the range of molecules a Third Eye ability can manipulate decreases as the range gets longer?"

"Ooh, that's pretty sharp for you, D&D. Maybe I really should start calling you AD&D..."

"I told you to cut that out!"

The argument that was about to break out between the chair on the far left of the line and the one on the right was interrupted by Suu's voice coming from the PC.

"I thought so, too."

The room quickly fell silent, and Suu's wispy voice echoed through it quietly.

"If this person could freely manipulate a protein insect inside a person's body, they wouldn't need to make the insects at all. They could just use the same proteins in the person's own body to attack the blood vessels of the heart or brain to kill them."

This frightful concept expressed in Suu's innocent voice gave even the Professor pause along with the others.

A few seconds later, the Professor unfolded her arms and spoke in an uncharacteristically strained voice.

"That's certainly true... With one exception, all the Third Eye abilities we know of are based on manipulating either molecular motion or molecular bonds through a mysterious means that we call the seventh force. If this person could continue manipulating these insects made of protein inside another human body, it would only make sense if they could do the same with the very proteins that make up the human body itself."

"Um...what is the 'one exception'?"

The Professor, Yumiko, DD, and Olivier all raised their eyebrows at Minoru's question.

"Oh...erm..."

"Isn't it obvious, Utsugi? She's talking about you."

"Ah..."

Yumiko's words prompted a memory in Minoru's mind. Now that she mentioned it, he felt as if the Professor had told him something similar before.

Professor Riri Isa chuckled, puttering over toward Minoru in her slippers.

"Yes, of course it's you, Mikkun. Your protective shell isn't a substance or a force field. And as of today, there's yet another mystery about it..."

"A-another...? Oh..."

Minoru trailed off, realizing what she meant. Most likely, the Professor was referring to the incident in which the protective shell restored Suu Komura's consciousness.

In that moment, Minoru did feel as if some kind of presence had made contact with the two of them from inside the shell. But thinking back on it now, he thought it might've just been a hallucination brought on by his desperate plea to his deceased sister Wakaba. Suu had already been recovered enough to send a Morse code message with her finger, after all. Even if Minoru hadn't brought her inside his shell, she might very well have woken up at the same time...

As if detecting Minoru's train of thought, the Professor smiled knowingly.

"There's no point in denying it now, Mikkun. Hinako said she felt something inside the shell, too."

"Wait...really?"

"Once she's discharged, I'd like to interview the both of you. But right now, we should be focusing on Red Coat's ability..."

Her smile fading, the Professor turned away and walked back to the monitor.

Feeling someone's gaze on the left side of his face, Minoru turned to look. Yumiko's eyes met his for just an instant, but she immediately turned back toward the front, so he couldn't tell what she'd been thinking.

"Just as DD said, this Ruby Eye's power contradicts a fundamental principle of Third Eye abilities…or so it would seem."

Since the Professor had started talking again, Minoru tried to concentrate on her words.

"But in the end, that principle is only based on our experience. All it really means is that the abilities of the Third Eye holders within the scope of our knowledge seemed to follow that pattern. If some parameter of the host, or perhaps the Third Eye itself, were particularly high, it may be possible to break that rule. But for now, we have to assume that there's still some restriction that prevents this Ruby Eye from manipulating the bodies of others, even though their ability can control the insects they create from a distance."

"Okay, sure, but…"

Olivier looked down at his right hand as if remembering something.

"It's dangerous to underestimate a Ruby's ability, y'know? We've already paid the price for that against both Igniter and Trancer."

"Yes…you're right, of course. From now on, we'll upgrade our assessment of Red Coat's ability and assume that control of our bodies isn't necessarily outside its scope. But as of now, based on what we've seen with the attacks on Mikkun and the hospital staff, it seems as if the spinebugs are the only…well, one of the only means of attacking anyway. There is actually one other kind of insect…"

The Professor tapped on the tablet, displaying a new picture on the monitor.

The image showed what looked like string coiled on a glossy ceramic tile floor. Minoru quickly realized what it was.

"Ah, that's…the wire that was used to tie up my legs and pull the Ruby Eye around. It's…it's an insect, too?"

"So it would seem, although its structure is simpler than the spinebugs'. It's made up of strands of an incredibly fine, 0.1 denier high-polymer fiber, twisted together to form a wire rope three millimeters thick. Dr. Nitamizu said it would be virtually impossible to cut without a specialized tool or some kind of ability. He's analyzing the molecular composition of the polymer as we speak."

"Denier…?" Minoru mumbled, quietly repeating an unfamiliar word from the Professor's explanation.

Tugging on the fabric of her black tights, Yumiko responded.

"It's a unit representing the thickness of a thread or string. The thread used for these tights is sixty deniers thick, so 0.1 denier would be mind-bogglingly thin."

"I—I see…"

Realizing that he'd reflexively been staring at Yumiko's tights, Minoru hurriedly looked away. The Professor grinned at this.

"Goodness, you're really going the extra mile, Yukko. I read somewhere that eighty denier is the standard for girls in winter."

"I-I'm not doing anything extra! I'm just a little more immune to the cold because of the Third Eye, that's all!"

"I see. Pardon me, then. Anyway, back to the matter at hand… This wire, which Red Coat created, has a structure very similar to human muscle fibers at its center, which can expand and contract freely. In other words, this is another pseudo-living creature. The doctor is calling it 'wireworm.' So to sum it up… Red Coat's Ruby Eye ability as we know it so far consists of firing two types of artificial insects from the left hand and controlling them: spinebugs, which explode, and wireworms, which are used for movement and restraints. Both seem to be designed solely for efficiently killing or capturing people in mind."

DD gave a little "hmm," lost in thought about the Professor's explanation.

"So…this person's not concerned about the method of killing, either…"

"That's right. Most likely, Red Coat doesn't particularly care about whether the insects come into play. If they had a handgun with a suppressor, they would probably use it without hesitation. Like a venomous insect… And so!"

The Professor manipulated the tablet again, then slapped a hand against the large monitor.

"For now, let's call this Ruby Eye—Identified Ruby Eye Host No. 30—by the temporary code name Stinger!"

Minoru stared intently at the security camera image on the screen.

The Ruby Eye in the red coat, standing in the darkness of the entrance hall, leaning forward slightly. Most likely, this was from the moment the murderer leaned down to look at Minoru. Due to the high position of the camera, the face was still hidden under the hood, and even the right half of the Ruby Eye's body couldn't be seen.

As he looked at the image, Minoru felt the memories of the battle prickling in his mind. Again, he had the feeling that he was forgetting something. Minoru bit his lip.

However, before he could come up with the source of the feeling, Olivier shouted something on his right.

"Stinger, huh? Finally, a new face! C'mon, D&D, let's go on patrol tonight!"

Immediately, DD and the Professor shouted in response.

"Idiot! You're so bandaged up, you're practically a mummy!"

"He's right, you fool! Get yourself back to the hospital now!"

"…Geez, can't a guy be a little pumped without getting yelled at…?"

Minoru smiled wryly, trying to console Olivier, who was sulking childishly and fidgeting with his glasses.

"Oli-V, you already did plenty of fighting at the hospital. Thank you again for your help… Now, please go rest so your wounds can heal, and leave the rest to us."

"Ah, Mikkun…you're the only nice person around here…"

With his exaggerated lament, Olivier reached out his right hand and clapped Minoru's shoulder lightly.

"But for real, I'm counting on you, Mikkun. As of right now, you're the only person who we know for sure can defend against that creep's insect attacks."

Minoru put his left hand over Olivier's—the same hand that had punched Minoru in the past—and nodded resolutely.

"Got it. We'll definitely catch him next time."

Yumiko and DD nodded in agreement with his declaration. Even Suu's quiet voice chimed in through the laptop on the table.

"I'll be back soon, too, so please wait just a little longer."

It was an uncharacteristically decisive statement for Suu. Yumiko nodded.

"Yes, please do come back quickly, Komura. You're the SFD's best forward."

For that moment, Minoru felt as though all five of them, including the absent Suu, were united by the same feelings.

Then a tinny, upbeat ringtone loudly filled the air. "Whoops, sorry," the Professor apologized, reaching into the pocket of her lab coat. She put the phone to her ear briskly. "Yes, this is Isa."

After a brief moment, the Professor's face froze, and a tremble ran through her tiny frame.

"Understood. I'll be waiting for the follow-up report."

Hanging up the phone, the Professor turned toward the other four, who were staring at her uncertainly, and moved her lips soundlessly as if searching for the right words. When she finally spoke, her voice shook tremulously.

"...That was a report from Dr. Nitamizu. They've finished the autopsy of the six Special Task Squad agents who were killed at the Syndicate base."

As soon as he heard that, Minoru's blood ran cold, and he breathed in sharply.

"...All six people had holes in the eardrums of their left or right ears, and their inner ears and brain stems were destroyed from the inside. And when they double-checked the helmets from their combat suits, they found tiny holes in the ventilation slit filters."

6

"Er…thank you for dinner and everything."

Getting out of the car, Ryuu Mikawa ducked his head to face Liquidizer, who leaned toward him from the Swift's driver's seat.

"Yes, I quite enjoyed it myself. I believe it's fairly likely that you'll be called in for that memory check soon enough, so do let me know if you hear anything."

"Sure. I appreciate your help with that."

"Not at all. Well, au revoir."

Liquidizer waved her left hand lightly before grasping the shift lever. Mikawa took a step back, and the white Swift took off smoothly, slipping in among the traffic along Kannana Road.

After treating him to *okonomiyaki* in Odaiba, Liquidizer had ended up insisting on driving him back to Ota Ward. Mikawa was now standing in front of the Keikyu Heiwajima Station, just ten minutes' walk north from the apartment where he lived alone. Technically, Oomorimachi would've been closer, but just in case—Ruby Eyes were nothing if not precautious—he decided against having her bring him to the closest station.

Of course, since Liquidizer had already tracked Mikawa down to the cold-storage warehouse in Ooi Futo, the place he most wanted to keep secret, this was probably a meaningless effort. If anything, she had probably long since figured out where he lived by now.

However, even if that were the case, he wanted to at least demonstrate that he wasn't willing to reveal his location so easily. Liquidizer was his benefactor, his former teacher, and had even treated him to *okonomiyaki*, but in the end, they were still both murderous Ruby Eyes. Members of the Syndicate were forbidden from fighting among themselves, but nevertheless, there was no telling when they might end up trying to kill one another.

If nothing else, he was fairly certain that Liquidizer would kill him without hesitation if she deemed it necessary, and Mikawa himself had a certain line that he would let no one cross, too. If anybody tried to disrupt OO's sleep in the pillar of ice inside that cold-storage warehouse, he would have to kill them, no matter who it might be.

……*That's right. Kill.*

A voice seemed to whisper from just behind Mikawa's head. His instinct was to turn and look behind him, but he didn't bother.

There was no one there. This was the voice of the parasitic Third Eye inside of Mikawa. Or more accurately, it was his brain translating the murderous impulses brought on by the Third Eye into a voice.

It was only six days ago that Mikawa killed seven people in the major accident at the Akasaka crossing. So he would still be able to ignore the voice for a while longer.

But after ten days or so, the voice would become increasingly vexing. And after twelve days, he would feel an overwhelming thirst, like his insides were turning to sand...and then he would kill again. It didn't matter who. He just had to unleash the power building within him, turning muddy water to pristine ice and extinguishing the flame of life.

It was no lie when he told his former teacher that he wanted to see the entire planet frozen over—Snowball Earth. If the entire world were to be covered in pure-white ice and everything ceased to move, he imagined it would be calm beyond words.

But at the same time, he couldn't help but wonder. Was this longing truly his own...or was it a fake feeling, planted by the Third Eye to motivate him to kill?

Tugging the zipper of his jacket up to his neck, Mikawa shoved both hands into his pockets as he walked along the path below the elevated railway, his thoughts spinning out of his control.

What if...

What if it had been a black Third Eye that entered Mikawa's body instead of a red one?

Would he be striving against the Ruby Eyes as one of the black hunters...the "SFD"? Standing side by side with the likes of Divider, Accelerator, and that ashen-haired Isolator...?

"...No, of course not."

Mikawa snorted bitterly.

Before the Third Eyes, he had already killed one person...or at least, suspended their life-sustaining activities.

On that day six years ago, Mikawa was the one who invited OO along.

At that time, Mikawa and OO were both victims of abuse, the former from his mother and the latter from her father. But while Mikawa's mother had abandoned all pretense of taking care of him, OO 's abuse was sexual in nature, and her mother was either unaware or ignoring the situation completely. After OO confided in him, Mikawa sent several anonymous e-mails to the child services center about it. But when the center finally conducted an investigation, because OO's father had a good reputation and a well-respected occupation, it was perfunctory at best and ended quickly.

And so, Mikawa and OO decided to escape to the future.

As a cold rain fell, they once again entered the frigid warehouse. This time, they had no plans of running away, no matter how cold it got.

Cold sleep. Mikawa had read about it in a book, and the two of them intended to carry it out. When they next woke up, they would be in a far-off future, in an ideal society where no adult would ever mistreat a child… They truly believed that.

Why was only Mikawa found right away and not OO?

He still didn't understand how it had happened. When he woke up, Mikawa was in the break room of the storage warehouse, where he was wrapped in a warm blanket and given a cup of hot cocoa. The staff, perhaps afraid of getting the police involved, let him off with a light scolding of "Don't sneak into places again!" and so Mikawa gave up and went home.

Naturally, OO's disappearance became a massive incident, with the mass media paying frequent visits to their school. Since Mikawa was close with OO, her parents—her father was sobbing, his eyes red—and the police all questioned him up and down, but he simply stated each time that he didn't know anything.

Mikawa had failed, but OO would go on to the future and find happiness there. A year passed, then two, and the investigation faded into obscurity, but Mikawa still believed that.

It was three years later that he finally learned that humans can't enter cold sleep just by being frozen.

Water increases in volume as it freezes. Due to this obvious phenomenon, the cells in a human being's body would be destroyed in the process, and even if thawed, they would never wake again.

In the present, deep down, Mikawa already knew the truth. OO wasn't sleeping in that pillar of ice in the warehouse…she had died the moment her body froze over.

However, her death would truly be final if that ice were to melt.

It had to stay frozen forever. If the entire earth were to freeze, not just the warehouse, and an eternal ice age spread stillness over the planet… Couldn't OO stay on the threshold between life and death forever…?

Truly, it was fate that gave Mikawa a red Third Eye and not a black one.

If he'd been a Jet Eye, he would never have joined the Syndicate or learned of their plan for human extinction. He was still a lowly member and didn't know the full story behind the organization or where its headquarters were located, but he would carry out his duties, rise through the ranks, and someday become an executive. Then he would induce the Syndicate to adopt Snowball Earth as the means for its human extinction plan. To do that, he would use Liquidizer or even betray her if the need arose.

Yet despite all that determination, he felt the fervor inside him growing dimmer.

It was only because the heat at the *okonomiyaki* room was too high. With that decided, Mikawa quickened his pace. Above his head, the high-speed train passed on the rails with a roar.

* * *

It was six o'clock on the dot when the meeting at SFD Headquarters ended.

The night had already grown pitch-dark outside the windows that lined the south wall of the room, and the glow of lights from Shinjuku twinkled beyond the trees in Toyama Park.

He had already told Norie that he was "visiting an injured friend," so he was probably still good on time. If he left now, he would be home by seven thirty.

With that in mind, Minoru took out his smartphone to text Norie his estimated arrival time. But before he could touch the screen, the Professor called to him from the lab area.

"Sorry, Mikkun, but could I have a little more of your time?"

Yumiko's voice followed shortly thereafter.

"I have business with you, too, Utsugi... Something I'd like to consult with you about, I suppose..."

"Oh...s-sure..."

Minoru glanced quickly at his phone before nodding. This must have conveyed his thoughts to Yumiko, who was quick to add, "I'll take you home on my motorcycle."

"Oh...um..."

If Yumiko gave him a lift on her beloved Agusta F3, it would shorten the length of his commute home significantly. But if, by chance, she was to use her acceleration ability, Minoru's ride in the tandem seat would be ten times more terrifying than any roller coaster.

Still, thinking about it, he realized this was probably the first time Yumiko had wanted his advice on anything. They'd fought together many times as a duo, too, and Minoru had the feeling that she wouldn't appreciate it if he said he just wanted to get home and eat dinner.

"Okay, then, if it's all right with you."

Minoru ducked his head, and the Professor beckoned again.

"All right, let's get our business over with first, then. What? It won't take long."

"Oh, um, right..."

Minoru hastened over to the lab area, and the Professor pulled an incredibly bulky envelope out of a desk drawer and handed it to him.

"Here, this is for December."

"Erm... Wh-what is it?"

Tilting his head uncertainly, Minoru shook the contents of the unsealed envelope into his hand.

Whump! Out slid a thick stack of ten thousand–yen bills, more than Minoru had ever seen in his life.

There were two bundles wrapped in currency straps. In addition, he found two coins and a three-millimeter stack of banknotes with a rose seal.

"Wh...wha—?!"

Minoru held the stack away from himself as if it might explode, nearly throwing it onto the floor.

"What...what on earth is this?!"

"What do you mean? It's your salary for December. Or your remuneration, if you want to be technical about it."

"H…huh?!"

Minoru stiffened, unable to process the Professor's words, and Yumiko spoke up calmly behind him.

"Oh, I see. Utsugi's first paycheck is in cash since he just joined in December, is it?"

"Mm-hmm. Starting in January, it'll be deposited into your own confidential bank account, so this is the only time you'll be paid in paper money like this. Feel free to roll around in a bed of it and such."

"I…I-I-I'm not going to do that! I mean…"

Minoru managed to calm himself down a little and pushed the roll of banknotes and coins back into the envelope. Then he offered it back to the Professor with both hands.

"…I can't accept this."

"Hmm? Why not?"

"Because…I promised Chief Himi. I told him I didn't need any money, just to borrow his ability once it's all over… That was my condition for fighting with the SFD. So I don't need this."

The Professor blinked at Minoru for a moment, then started to open her mouth.

But it was Yumiko, standing next to Minoru, who spoke up first.

"Are you sure that's quite accurate?"

"Um…accurate…?"

"I was right there when you and Chief Himi had that conversation. And I distinctly remember you asking if there would be some kind of reward when the Ruby Eye situation is resolved."

"R…right…"

"And the chief responded that when the SFD is disbanded, its members will be paid in recognition for their services. I was told the same thing, but that bonus is like a completion bonus or severance pay, completely unrelated to monthly recompense. In other words, you only relinquished your final bonus, so I believe you ought to accept your monthly salary as per the norm. I'm sure Chief Himi expects the same."

"What…? No, but…"

Minoru stammered for a while before coming up with a rebuttal.

"I mean, I wasn't expecting there to be a monthly salary at all! Why would I? Especially not one as large as this!"

This time it was the Professor who countered him.

"No, if anything, why *wouldn't* you expect a salary?"

"What do you…?"

"All our members, including you, Mikkun, put their lives on the line to battle Ruby Eyes. When you fought against Biter, Igniter, and Liquidizer and Trancer, you narrowly escaped death each and every time. There's probably no occupation in modern Japan that requires people to work so closely with death as the SFD and the Self-Defense Forces' STS. And Sanako—that is, Sanae—is in a coma after falling into a state of brain death after an attack from Igniter. Do you really think anyone should be made to volunteer without pay for such a job?!"

The Professor's sharp words left Minoru at a loss.

She was probably right—at the very least, Sanae, who was still comatose in room 404, and the six elite STS agents who were killed in battle certainly deserved to be paid highly. And of course, he had no objection to Yumiko, DD, Olivier, and the others being paid for their dangerous work.

But I'm not…

Minoru looked at Yumiko and the Professor in turn before speaking.

"…I didn't join the SFD because I wanted to protect Japan, or save the world, or anything like that. I'm only here because of a selfish wish—to go to a world where no one knows who I am. I can't take all this money, I don't deserve…"

Yumiko physically prevented him from finishing his sentence, namely by suddenly pressing his mouth shut with her left hand.

"I beg your pardon, Utsugi. But your motivation doesn't matter. When I first met you, I foolishly told you that as a Jet Eye, you have an obligation to keep fighting until all the Ruby Eyes are gone… But I take that back. There's no such obligation to put your life on the line like this. And everyone has different abilities… If someone chooses not to fight, nobody has the right to judge them."

With that, Yumiko finally released Minoru's mouth. She pressed that hand to her chest instead, casting her eyes downward as she spoke.

"…It's not as though I'm fighting for some noble cause, either. To be quite honest, I think I'm fighting for much pettier reasons… My pride, my self-worth, my reason for living after being injured and losing the ability to run. And…for Sanae. So that she'll know that she doesn't have to worry about me anymore. But in the end, even that's just for my own satisfaction…"

"Yumiko…"

That's not true. I'm sure Sanae understands your feelings, Minoru wanted to say. But he couldn't do it. She knew better than anyone else that Sanae's consciousness was gone, lost when she fell to brain death, and that she was only still breathing at the will of her Third Eye.

"…But I still accept the money. And after the SFD dissolves, I'll need it to ensure that Sanae is cared for. If it will ease your conscience, then you should find one, too…a way to use it that isn't for yourself. There must be something you can think of."

Minoru's breath caught in his throat.

She was right, of course. The first thing that came to mind was strengthening the security at his home, and while Suu's brother and his "observing figures" were taking care of her right now, if Minoru had money, he could help with that, too.

Really, his adoptive sister Norie must have spent a great deal of money on raising Minoru for the past eight years. It made sense to save up now, even just to pay her back for that someday.

Minoru slowly lowered the envelope, which he'd still been holding at an arm's length, and Yumiko nodded with a little smile before furrowing her brow.

"Besides, that money probably includes the pay for when you went into the reactor core at the Tokyo Bay Nuclear Power Plant. Isn't that right, Professor?"

"Yes, that's about thirty percent of it."

"That seems much too small, don't you think?! I heard the development cost for that robot, that Loser or Muser or whatever, was over five hundred million yen. He should get a ten percent finder's fee at least—five million yen!"

"Five million…?!"

Minoru shook his head rapidly, but the Professor responded quite seriously.

"To be precise, it's stipulated in Article 28 of the Lost Items Act that the reward must be 'no less than five percent and no more than twenty percent' of the item's value, so the max would be one hundred million yen."

"One…hundred…"

"Oh, right, speaking of Muser... Ah, well, that can probably wait until next time."

Stopping just shy of saying something else, the Professor clapped her hands together vigorously, as if to say the matter was closed.

"Well then, we'll just say that Mikkun's recompense for next month will remain the same. To be clear, we SFD members aren't actually employees of the Ministry of Health, Labor, and Welfare but sole proprietors of an outside business, so the amount of our pay does fluctuate based on the work done in that month. Generally, you can think of each Ruby Eye case as around five hundred thousand yen."

"Really, doesn't that seem low? Our lives are on the line here!" Yumiko grumbled.

To Minoru, who was still in high school, even five hundred thousand yen sounded like a truly outrageous amount of money. Lifting the heavy envelope to his chest, he bowed his head to the Professor.

"No, no... This is more than enough. So...thank you very much."

"Of course. But don't just save it up for someone else—if you deem it necessary, you should most certainly use it for yourself. Ideally, that money is meant to be used so that you can better prepare yourselves for your duties."

"R...right."

Minoru wondered what he could possibly use this for as he nodded, but then Yumiko interjected again.

"Buy a motorcycle already. It'll make getting around much easier."

"A motorcycle...?!"

"Yes, excellent idea. It is possible to use the equipment budget to buy a vehicle if you keep it at headquarters, but if you want to keep it at home, you have to buy it with your own money, I'm afraid."

"B...but I don't even have a license." Minoru hurriedly cut in, getting the feeling that the two of them would get the better of him again if he let them keep discussing this without him. However, Yumiko promptly responded with some new information.

"Oh, the SFD can take care of that in no time. Though, of course, I'm a highly skilled driver already."

"......Well, if I decide to buy one, I'll be sure to ask about it, then..."

Managing to escape that topic for the time being, Minoru put the envelope at the bottom of his messenger bag. Thinking that he didn't want to walk around with nothing but that stack of money in his bag, Minoru suddenly had an idea.

"Oh, right, I should bring the containers home… Excuse me a moment."

Minoru started to walk toward the kitchen area, but Yumiko suddenly accelerated forward and grabbed his shoulder at breakneck speed.

"Containers? What containers?"

"Oh, um…I brought mochi from home, so…"

"Mochi?!"

Yumiko's face became far more serious than it had been during the conversation about money, and her tone made it sound like a cross-examination.

"If there was more than one container, that means it wasn't just pre-packaged mochi slices, correct?"

"Y-yeah. They were soy flour, seaweed wrapped, and cheese, I think…"

"…!! Don't tell me you and the Professor ate them for lunch?"

"Well, we did, but…there should be more left, I think…"

"I'll have some."

With that curt declaration, Yumiko shot over to the kitchen, yanking Minoru along by the arm. Along the way, she paused to look at the blanketed table in front of the TV and nodded triumphantly.

"I knew it! I was wondering why there was a *kotatsu* out here. So this must be the scene of the crime…"

"Wh-what crime?! …I'll heat the mochi up, so you can just wait here, all right…?"

"Oh, really? Don't mind if I do, then!"

Minoru headed to the kitchen on the other side of the lab area, leaving Yumiko to dive gleefully under the heated table.

He retrieved the three containers from the German-made refrigerator—rumor had it that DD, who enjoyed cooking, had purchased it with SFD funds—and heated up the soy flour mochi in the microwave, using the water oven to heat the other two kinds. Since there were only two of each left, he arranged them on one long bisque platter and carried it over to Yumiko along with some tea.

Yumiko was already nestled snugly under the *kotatsu* watching the news on TV, and her face lit up like a child's when the mochi was placed before her eyes. After agonizing over the decision of which to try first for a moment, she placed a cheese mochi onto her plate and barely uttered a quick "Thanks" before taking a huge bite.

"Hot, hot...! Oh, this is excellent, though. This mochi was made with a mortar and pestle, wasn't it?"

"Y-yeah... How can you tell?"

"The stretchiness and mouthfeel is quite different from pounded mochi..." Yumiko looked at him suspiciously. "Wait, aren't you the one who brought them in, Utsugi?"

"Oh yeah, but..."

Minoru was about to explain that he'd gotten them from Minowa's family, but he quickly stopped himself. Yumiko knew Tomomi Minowa from the time that the latter had almost become the Biter's victim, of course, and had seen Minoru talking to Minowa near their school. So she would presumably recognize the name...but for some reason, Minoru had a gut feeling that he'd be better off not mentioning that part.

"...I actually got it at a f-friend's house. Apparently, they get them from family in the countryside every year, but I didn't know that they were made with a pestle, that's all..."

"...Your voice sounds a bit unnatural right now, don't you think?"

"I—I—I don't know what you mean. I'll have one, too, if you don't mind."

With that, Minoru quickly grabbed one of the seaweed-wrapped mochi and took a huge bite.

Yumiko was still looking at him suspiciously, but in the end her hunger won out, and she put the rest of her cheese mochi into her mouth with her left hand even as she reached her chopsticks toward the soy flour mochi with her right.

After Yumiko decimated the five mochi in a matter of minutes, she sipped on the tea with a contented expression, so Minoru inwardly breathed a sigh of relief. Then he remembered something.

"Come to think of it, didn't you want to talk to me about something?"

"Oh...yes. I thought we'd do it in my room, but... Well, this should be fine."

Yumiko glanced at the lab area on her right. Once she confirmed the ongoing sound of the Professor's ultra-high-speed typing, she turned back toward Minoru.

"I wanted to consult with you...about Sanae."

"Huh? Miss Ikoma...?"

Minoru drew back a little in surprise at the unexpected name.

Sanae Ikoma, code name Shooter, was an SFD member who had originally been Yumiko's partner in battle. She was said to have brought in many a Ruby Eye with her bow and her powerful combat-based Third Eye ability, which allowed her to hit any target that she could see, but Igniter's oxygen deprivation attack had caused her permanent brain damage.

Apparently, both the NCAM's diagnosis and the Professor's judgment with her speculation ability had concluded that there was no possibility that Sanae would ever wake from her coma. But Sanae was still sleeping in room 404 of headquarters, and Yumiko had just said earlier that she was prepared to care for her after the SFD disbanded.

What could she possibly want to "consult" with Minoru about regarding Sanae...?

Minoru held his breath and waited for Yumiko to continue. She leaned just a little closer to him before speaking.

"Utsugi, your ability...your protective shell...has many characteristics that are still shrouded in mystery, even to you."

"Huh...? Well, yes..."

"So I won't ask for any concrete evidence. I just want to know your... feelings, your instinct... about what I'm going to ask you."

With this mysterious introduction, Yumiko brought her serious face even closer to Minoru and whispered her question.

"Do you think it's possible if you bring Sanae into your shell...that she might wake up, like Komura did?"

"......!!"

It was a question that had never even occurred to Minoru in the slightest before.

But in Yumiko's position, it was only natural that she would ask it.

Something...or someone...had touched Suu Komura's head when she was gravely wounded and inside his protective shell. Minoru had felt it. If he had to put it into words, it was like a young child, nervously reaching out to make contact with an unknown being...

Minoru had explained this sensation to the Professor and Yumiko at the hospital in Hiroo. And immediately after waking up, Suu also said that she had felt something touch her head.

So if he brought Sanae Ikoma into the protective shell, perhaps that unknown force might heal her, too. More likely than not, Yumiko had been thinking about it since the moment Suu regained consciousness.

Above all, Minoru had to answer this question completely truthfully and sincerely.

Closing his eyes, he tried to call back the memory of what he felt at that moment. At the same time, he once again thought about the mysterious power of his protective shell.

"……I think……"

When he finally spoke, it was so faint that even Minoru himself couldn't hear it. He took a deep breath, steadied himself, and tried again, a little louder this time.

"…I think…there might be a possibility. At the very least, I can't say for sure that there isn't…"

Yumiko caught her breath sharply.

Minoru knew that he might be giving her nothing but false hope. But this was also how he honestly felt.

"…I think the inside of the protective shell is more than just a tiny space protected by a barrier. I can hear that strange echoing sound, and I never run out of oxygen inside… It's a little frightening to think about it, to be honest, but if there's something in there that I can't see, making that noise and providing oxygen…and if it's the same something that woke Suu up, then maybe it would heal anyone inside the shell…at least, that's the feeling I get. Although I don't have any basis for it…"

"……I see. Hmm… All right…"

Yumiko nodded slowly, as if reflecting on Minoru's every word.

Then Minoru asked her a question of his own.

"Um, there's something I wanted to ask you, too… When we fought Igniter at Ariake Heaven's Shore and again when we fought Liquidizer at the factory in Minami-Aoyama…you came into my protective shell. Did you…feel anything when you were in there with me? Like there was another presence there besides just us, for example…?"

"……Hmm…"

Now Yumiko looked down at the surface of the *kotatsu*, her expression complicated, as if she were searching her memories.

After a moment, she shook her head without looking up.

"...To be honest, both times I was only thinking about the enemy in front of us... I didn't have time to feel or think about anything else. I don't even remember whether I heard the sound you mentioned."

"I see..."

"But the one thing I do remember is... In both cases, we were fighting for our lives, but when I was in the shell, I felt safe. How should I put it...? As if I was being protected...? ...Well, I guess that's pretty obvious."

With that, Yumiko smiled a little.

In the moment he saw that smile, Minoru made a suggestion that even he wasn't expecting.

"Um...would you like to try the experiment again?"

"Huh? What experiment...?"

"The experiment of bringing you into the protective shell. It never worked when we did it here before, but I think maybe...right now..."

Yumiko blinked a few times, then looked away, a little flustered.

"Ah...y-yes, well, you might be right. I do have the same feeling, I suppose."

"Then why don't we get the Professor and..."

Minoru started to stand up, but Yumiko raised her left hand to stop him, gesturing for him to sit back down.

"But no, let's not do it right now. If we fail again now, I don't think I'll be able to recover."

"......All right..."

Minoru sat back down on the cushion, gathering his thoughts for a moment before looking up.

"...Sorry for making such a strange suggestion. Anyway, to get back to the main subject..."

"N-no, it's all right. I was rather happy that you suggested it... Oh, sorry, go ahead."

Yumiko still looked a bit flustered, so Minoru gave her a moment to calm down before he continued.

"...Like I said before, I do think it's possible that something could happen if I bring Sanae into the shell. But what worries me is that I can't guarantee that it'll definitely be a positive phenomenon... Not to mention, we don't know whether I can actually even bring her inside."

"Oh..."

Yumiko looked as if that possibility hadn't occurred to her.

"But Sanae is sleeping. No matter how close you get to her, there will be absolutely no response. You still don't think it would work?"

"Um..."

Minoru searched for the words to properly explain.

"...Um, for a long time, I thought the protective shell was the embodiment of rejection... That the Third Eye had given me an impenetrable barrier so that I could reject everything around me. But...after I brought you into the shell and then Suu, I've realized that I might've been wrong."

"About what...?"

"Everything. I think the protective shell might be the opposite of rejection... Um, it's hard to say it without sounding weird, but maybe it's something like...affection...?"

Minoru paused for a moment, bracing himself for Yumiko to object.

However, the girl in the blazer made no move to speak right away and instead pushed both her hands under the *kotatsu* quilt.

She seemed to be stretching her legs out underneath; the tip of one small toe even touched Minoru's right foot. But Yumiko didn't seem to notice, and her long silence continued.

The light sound of the Professor tapping away at her keyboard continued from the lab area. On the large television, the weather forecast portion of the news program began; the weatherman warned of cold with exaggerated gestures.

"Affection...," Yumiko muttered unexpectedly. "...I think I understand what you mean. There was nothing harsh or prickly about the inside of your shell. Like I said earlier, it felt as if I was being completely protected...a gentle, calming place... But if that's the case...doesn't that mean it would have no reason to reject Sanae...?"

"...I don't think my feelings alone are enough."

"What...?"

"I think I have to be sort of in sync with the person I'm trying to bring inside... Um, this is going to sound really corny, but it's like—our hearts have to become one or something. In the hospital, when I brought Suu inside the shell...it seemed like she was in a coma, but her heart was still open somehow. It was like she felt our presence through the glass, and she was just aware enough to send the Morse code message. But in Sanae's case…"

Minoru fell silent, unable to bring himself to complete the statement.

Instead, Yumiko filled in the rest in a painful voice.

"…Sanae's heart is completely closed off… I was her partner, and even I can't feel her presence there. So it's probably too much to ask you to try to do the same…"

"…Of course, I can't say for sure that it would fail. For all we know, if I tried to bring her into my shell, it could succeed easily. But…if it does fail, Sanae's body will be thrown violently out of the shell. And I think the shock might be bad enough to negatively affect her condition…"

"……"

Yumiko said nothing for a while.

Minoru tried to look away, unable to watch her expression as she fought off a wave of grief. But as he turned, he caught a glimpse of the small tears trembling on her long eyelashes.

He watched helplessly as the two droplets grew until they finally fell from her lashes onto the surface of the *kotatsu*.

"…If…if you'd been a member of the SFD back then, too…"

Her lips trembled a little as she spoke softly.

"…You and Sanae would have gotten along, I think. You're both shy yet surprisingly stubborn… If only you'd been friends, you might be able to bring her into the shell, even while she's unconscious…"

For a moment, Yumiko's feet moved under the *kotatsu* to press against Minoru's right leg.

Then, after staying like that for a few seconds, Yumiko slowly pulled her legs out and stood up. Brushing off her skirt lightly, the Accelerator's expression returned to its usual cool smile as she looked back at Minoru.

"…I'm sorry for taking up so much of your time. I'll take you to Saitama now."

✳ ✳ ✳

As he neared his apartment, Mikawa relaxed his pace a little.

Staring at the curved mirror at the intersection in front of him, he checked carefully that there were no suspicious shadows behind him.

At the same time, he inhaled slowly, making sure he didn't smell the presence of any black Third Eyes. It was a routine that he always practiced on his way home; he had never been tailed yet, but Liquidizer once said that these kinds of precautions could make the difference between life and death.

Indeed, earlier today, Liquidizer herself had followed Mikawa into the cold-storage warehouse in Ooi Futo without his noticing. If that had been an SFD agent instead of his former master, Mikawa would be dead or captured by now—and even if he did manage to escape, OO would still have been discovered.

Confirming that he was safe, Mikawa turned the last corner. Before long, he could see the ordinary, two-story wood apartment building on the right side of the street. Mikawa was renting room 201, the corner room at the front of this building, so he would be able to see if there were any lights inside before he entered the building.

Everything seemed normal as usual, but just to be sure, he took his final precautionary measure. He stopped at the very edge of where his apartment's wireless signal would reach and took his smartphone out of his jacket pocket. Connecting to the network, he brought up the real-time feed from the webcam he had installed inside.

Nothing out of the ordinary.

Now confident that everything was safe, Mikawa headed up the stairs to his apartment. As he took the key ring out of his jeans pocket and brought the dimple key up to the doorknob, he made an annoying mistake that happened occasionally: The titanium chain attached to the key ring was pulled too tightly, tugging on the body piercing on the left side of his waist.

"Ugh…"

Reflexively, Mikawa twisted to the side to ease the unpleasant sensation of his skin being pulled tight.

It was this unintentional movement that saved Mikawa's life.

At that exact moment, there was the faint sound of something whizzing through the air, and a flying object grazed Mikawa's neck and lodged itself in the door before his eyes.

"……?!"

Though he was now in high-alert mode, Mikawa's line of sight was drawn for a moment to the object that had stabbed itself into the door.

At first, he thought it was an insect, but he'd never seen one like this before.

It was no larger than seven millimeters. The head tapered off into a needle-like tip, which was wedged into the plywood door. The swollen rear section of its body lacked the six legs of an insect and was instead covered in tiny hairs, which were squirming about like the feelers of a sea anemone.

If he hadn't been bent to the side, this insect might have stabbed into Mikawa's neck instead of the door.

This didn't look like any insect that was native to Japan. Was it an invasive pest from another country...? It seemed like the bloodsucking type, too.

Mikawa's face wrinkled up in disgust, and he reached out a finger of his right hand, meaning to crush the bug that was lodged in the door.

Just then, he felt the tiny hairs on the nape of his neck bristling.

What if this was no mere pest but a man-made object? If it was a living weapon created by a Third Eye ability...?

Mikawa turned sharply on the spot.

In front of the two-story apartment building was a one-way street, on the other side of which was a four-story building with larger apartments. It looked about as old as Mikawa's cheap building, and its spray-painted walls were cracked and stained in several places.

And between the second and third floors of that apartment complex... Someone was standing on the outer staircase, illuminated faintly by the fluorescent lights.

Whoever it was, they weren't very tall. Because of the obstructing wall, Mikawa could only see them from the chest up, but it was impossible to gauge their age or gender. The hood of the red coat they wore was pulled deep over their face, shrouding it in total darkness.

Silently, the figure raised their left hand.

The fluorescent light glinted off something metal in the center of the person's gloved palm.

There was neither sound nor flash, but Minoru could sense with his eyes, ears, and even his skin that something had fired out of it.

It wasn't a gun, a crossbow, or anything of the sort. It was an ability. The person in the red coat had to be an enemy—someone who possessed a black Third Eye.

The extremely small object flew toward Mikawa in an S-shaped arc. If the enemy was controlling its path, then there was no chance he could dodge it this time.

His lungs full of air that he'd been sucking in as he searched for the enemy, Mikawa let it all out in a thin, sharp breath.

The flying object—probably the same as the strange insect lodged in the door behind him—was surrounded by glittering air. Mikawa's transition ability had turned the moisture in the air into ice.

However, it was January at present. The weather had been clear since New Year's, and the snow from that New Year's Eve had melted away, so the air was getting dry. It couldn't be more than 30 percent humidity.

As a result, the supercooling effect that Mikawa produced wasn't enough to encase the insect in ice and bring it to the ground.

However, it did freeze enough to slow the flying bug's impact, so even if he couldn't dodge it completely, it bought Mikawa just enough time to defend himself.

He threw his left hand up to protect his neck and felt a light impact and a stabbing pain at the base of his thumb and forefinger.

About two centimeters below the frozen portion, the revolting insect had stabbed deeply into his hand. Not only that, but it was using its countless tiny hairs to turn itself around, burrowing into his skin like a drill.

"Shit…!" Mikawa swore as he tried to catch the insect with his right hand.

He just barely managed to dig a nail into it and yanked it out with all his might, causing an unpleasant ripping in his flesh, as if the thing were covered in tiny spikes.

Quickly, Mikawa crushed the struggling insect between his fingers. The rounded part of the body gave way with a snap, releasing an unpleasant-smelling liquid that stuck to his fingers.

Mikawa grimaced with revulsion, then looked up to see that the red-coated person on the stairs across the street was raising their left hand toward him again.

It seemed like they couldn't rapid-fire the insects continuously, but if the shots kept coming, sooner or later Mikawa wouldn't be able to protect himself. The insects were incredibly small, only about seven millimeters long, but it would surely still be trouble if one of them penetrated deep enough into his body.

Mikawa had no choice. He had to use his trump card.

Quickly, he moved his right hand behind his back, pulling out a small two hundred–milliliter plastic bottle from the pocket of his shoulder bag.

All that was inside was water. But for Ryuu Mikawa, the Trancer, it was the ultimate weapon of both attack and defense. Really, he would prefer to carry around a two-liter bottle at all times, but it would be too bulky and was likely to invoke suspicion if the police were to question him.

Mikawa didn't hesitate as he threw the bottle—his lifeline—across the street.

The distance from where he stood to the stairs of the apartment complex across the road was about eighteen meters. With the powerful arm of a Ruby Eye, it would be possible to throw it across in a straight line at that distance, but Mikawa took a chance and tossed the bottle in a loose arc.

A moment later, the red-coated person also launched three insects from their left hand, then crouched down immediately. They were probably trying to take cover behind the wall of the stairs, but that wouldn't be enough to avoid Trancer's secret weapon.

Aiming at the plastic bottle, Mikawa let out all the air in his lungs in a thick breath.

Instantly, the two hundred milliliters of water in the bottle turned into steam.

When water turns into vapor, its volume increases to 1,700 times its initial size. Of course, this wouldn't fit inside a tiny bottle. And this wasn't a thin, pliable eco-bottle but an exceedingly thick plastic bottle from a particular foreign brand.

Just as it arrived at the stairs of the apartment complex, the bottle swelled up into a near perfectly spherical shape, then exploded with a bang as the casing gave way.

The pressure limit of the bottle Mikawa had thrown was about two megapascals. Once Mikawa superheated it, the steam's temperature exceeded two hundred degrees Celsius.

The high-temperature steam completely enveloped the stairs where the enemy was hiding. The force of the explosion reached all the way to Mikawa, easily blowing the flying insects away.

On top of that, the detonated bottle should have shattered into countless pieces, which would scatter like shrapnel. Mikawa didn't think that would be enough to kill the Jet Eye, of course, but it should buy him some time.

Shoving the key that was still in his left hand into his pocket, Mikawa jumped over the rail of the outside corridor and onto the road. The shock sent a tingle of pain through the wounds in his left shoulder and chest.

White mist was still hanging over the area. This was his only chance to escape. As Liquidizer's pupil, the thought of running away so easily peeved him, but the black hunters never acted alone. He didn't see anyone on the street, but there had to be at least one other enemy lurking somewhere. And the wound where Divider had cut him still hadn't healed completely.

The sounds of doors and windows opening echoed along the street, most likely people who were surprised by the sound of the explosion. After hesitating for just a moment, Mikawa started running east.

He could never return to that apartment again. Since Liquidizer had told him to be ready to abandon the place at a moment's notice, he hadn't left any valuable items or anything that would hint at his real identity. Nonetheless, in the three months that he'd been living in the apartment, he had started to feel somewhat comfortable there.

"...Damn it..."

Mikawa swore again as he ran at close to his top speed. He had just remembered the high-quality ice in his freezer that he'd just gone all the way to Koujiya to purchase. Of course, Mikawa could make that sort of thing himself, but he couldn't just use his ability at home, and there was a certain quality to ice from the old-fashioned ice shop that he couldn't quite replicate. He'd been looking forward to making shaved ice with it.

But this was no time to start thinking longingly about ice. He had to escape from the Jet Eyes on foot, while they might be using cars and motorcycles, and he still didn't know how they had found his home in the first place. He would have liked to escape to the Syndicate safe house in Gotanda, but he couldn't do that until he figured out how they had tracked him down.

Once he could shake off the enemy for sure, he would have to contact Liquidizer right away. As Mikawa's thoughts raced, he passed beneath the rails of the Keikyu main line.

Ahead was Route 1 across the Oomori overpass, then Heiwanomori Park, then Heiwajima Park. He should be able to tell there whether he was still being followed. And before he got there, he'd have to buy a bottle of water at a vending machine somewhere...

Mikawa subconsciously sniffed the air as his mind continued spinning.

He didn't smell the ether-like chemical smell of a Jet Eye. So at the very least, there was no enemy nearby using an ability. That red-coated attacker must have taken at least a bit of damage from the steam grenade...

At that moment, another thought occurred to him.

Suddenly realizing his major error, Ryuu Mikawa gasped. His legs tangled, and he just barely stopped himself from falling.

He didn't smell anything.

Not only just then—but when the enemy had attacked him at his apartment. He hadn't smelled the slightest whiff of a Jet Eye.

But that was impossible. Those insects were definitely created by a Third Eye ability, and it was less than eighteen meters away. Given how complex the ability was, since it could create and control artificial creatures from a distance, he should have been able to smell it from at least thirty meters away.

Unless... This could only mean one thing.

"...It's not a Jet Eye...?"

Mikawa unconsciously slowed his running speed.

If that attacker wasn't a new face from the Jet Eye organization, the SFD...

There was only one explanation. The attacker was a Ruby Eye, like Mikawa. Moreover, it was an independent Ruby Eye who didn't belong to the Syndicate.

He had just talked about this with Liquidizer at the *okonomiyaki* restaurant in Odaiba. The mysterious Ruby Eye known as X, who had been hiding out in the Keihinjima warehouse and easily killed the six members of the invading Self-Defense Force team.

And Liquidizer had said that X's main goal was likely not to kill the Self-Defense Forces personnel.

It was to kill their own kind.

A Ruby Eye that hunted other Ruby Eyes.

A shudder ran through Mikawa's body that couldn't be explained by the cold.

He stopped running and turned. The dimly lit road stretched in a straight line beyond the elevated tunnel he'd just passed beneath. There was no one else there—as far as he could see anyway.

But if the opponent was a Ruby, he wouldn't be able to detect them by their scent. Ruby Eyes generally didn't sense one another, even if one used an ability.

"......Shit!"

Gritting his teeth, Mikawa started running again. If he couldn't rely on his nose, all he had was his basic physical strength. Although the other Ruby Eye wouldn't smell it if Mikawa used his ability, there was a chance that it would actually draw the attention of Jet Eyes this time, and his transition ability was only really useful for movement on rainy days anyway.

As soon as he turned from the narrow street onto Route 1, Mikawa was hit with a flood of noise.

Cars flew by one after another on the side road and overpass, and there were at least ten pedestrians on the sidewalk that he could see.

However, this didn't assure his safety. The independent Ruby's attack was an assassination-type ability. Even if he were in sight of passersby, he could still be shot without hesitation.

Mikawa clearly wasn't dressed like a jogger, but he didn't have any control over that in this situation. Running just slowly enough so as to avoid drawing the attention of the ordinary pedestrians, he passed under the overhead bridge and headed along the east side of Route 1. For now, he just had to keep moving. That, and get in contact with Liquidizer.

He had pulled out his smartphone and was starting up the phone app as he ran when a possibility occurred to him that made his eyes widen.

If the person in the red coat was a Ruby Eye, it was possible that they had learned Mikawa's address through a Syndicate information leak.

And furthermore, it was possible that this leak was intentional.

It could be that, for whatever reason, the Syndicate was trying to dispose of Mikawa. It was even possible that Liquidizer was in on the plan.

Was it his former master who had sent the red-coated assassin after him?

Was appearing to him at the cold-storage warehouse and treating him to *okonomiyaki* her way of saying good-bye...?

Feeling more lost than he ever had since gaining the Third Eye, Mikawa desperately pushed more power into his legs and kept running.

7

Slowly walking west along the path through Toyama Park, Minoru heard the sound of a three-cylinder engine rapidly approaching from up ahead.

A black Agusta F3 800. The cowl shone like a mirror despite frequent use, and the screen was equally spotless.

Come to think of it, this motorcycle's Italian like the Alfa Romeo, isn't it? Minoru thought as he slowed to a halt. The motorcycle did an elegant U-turn around him and stopped as well.

Yumiko dismounted and set up the kickstand. She must have been rushing for Minoru's sake; instead of her usual leather getup, she was wearing a biker's jacket over her blazer and had simply added leg warmers up to her knees instead of changing into her pants. In other words, she was still wearing her uniform skirt.

"U-um…will you be all right speeding around in that…?"

"What, am I going to just take it off and drive without it?"

Minoru had no comeback for that as Yumiko pulled out his helmet, which had previously been used by Sanae Ikoma, from the rear case. Accepting it, Minoru stored his messenger bag where the helmet had been. Donning the helmet and turning on the built-in intercom and visor display, he promptly heard Yumiko's voice in his ear.

"All right, let's go. I'll treat you to an extra-special ride as thanks for the mochi."

"S-sure."

What does "extra-special" mean?! Minoru panicked inwardly. *She's not going to use her acceleration ability, is she…?* But it was too late to worry about that. Now that he was sitting on her monster machine, all he could do was trust his fate to the whims of the rider.

The Agusta started up easily. Then just as the gear changed from second to third—

"Yukko, Mikkun, are you still nearby?!"

Professor Riri Isa's voice burst out urgently from the intercom speakers.

"Yes, we're still in Toyama Park…"

"Thank goodness. There's been a 3E incident in Oomori West in Ota Ward! There was a small-scale explosion on the outside staircase of an

apartment complex, and two residents who went to see what happened were killed!"

"……!"

Yumiko's sharp gasp echoed through the speakers, and Minoru, hanging on to her on the motorcycle, felt her body tense.

"What was the MO?!"

Yumiko lowered the speed of the motorcycle as she asked, and the Professor hesitated for just a moment before responding.

"…They were both bleeding from one ear, with no other visible trauma. In other words, it's possible that it was the work of the assailant from NCAM—Stinger."

"What…?!"

This time it was Minoru who exclaimed with surprise.

"It was just after four o'clock that Stinger escaped from the hospital! There's already another incident not even three hours later…?!"

"If it really is Stinger, then yes, so it would seem… It's certainly not impossible to get to Ota Ward in three hours—by train, car, even on foot—but it seems too soon for them to take action again like this."

"Either way, we have to hurry! Utsugi, are you coming?"

There was no way that Minoru could refuse.

He'd end up getting home late at night or maybe not at all, and he'd have to lie to Norie, too—but as a Jet Eye and a member of the SFD, he had to do it.

"Yes, of course!"

As soon as he responded, Yumiko touched her helmet against his with a *clunk*.

"All right. Now hang on tight!"

"Right!"

Minoru nodded again, holding on to Yumiko with his arms and both knees.

The motorcycle's right turn signal went on as they made another U-turn. Then the pair darted along the winding path out of the park. As soon as the bike hit the broader main road, the flashing red patrol lights lit up on the rear case.

"Professor, please send me the location!"

In a matter of seconds, a full-color map appeared in the lower right corner of the visor display. In the center, a red dot marked their destination. Minoru wasn't very familiar with Ota Ward, but it seemed to be less than five kilometers northwest of Haneda Airport. Which meant...

"Huh...this is close to the place where the STS team was killed by Stinger, isn't it...?"

After a moment, the Professor's voice responded.

"...*You're right... I'm not sure whether it's a coincidence or not. We don't even know what the source of the explosion was... There's too little information.*"

"The victims this time weren't Third Eye holders, were they?"

As soon as Minoru asked the question, he realized that he already knew the answer.

"Oh, never mind, I'm sorry. You said the only external wound was bleeding from the ears."

"*Right. Since there was no exodus phenomenon, they must not have been Jet or Ruby Eyes. Therefore, I believe that they were simply caught up in the situation like the victims at the hospital, not targeted by Stinger.*"

"...In that case, it's possible that Stinger was targeting someone else—it could be a Jet Eye who the SFD hasn't discovered yet. So maybe the explosion was that person's ability...?"

The Professor didn't respond to Yumiko right away.

After several dozen seconds, as the motorcycle was turning onto Waseda Avenue, she finally spoke through the intercom in an uncharacteristically short tone.

"*...There's just not enough data yet. I can't say anything for certain. The Oomori police force is checking the security cameras in the area right now, but it is a residential area... As soon as we have more information, I'll let you know right away. DD is heading there from the hospital, too, but you'll probably get there first.*"

"Understood. We should be arriving at the scene in about...fifteen minutes."

Sitting in the tandem seat, Minoru was startled by Yumiko's response.

The expected arrival time displayed on the navigation screen of the visor display was more than forty minutes from now. The shortest route from Toyama in Shinjuku Ward to Oomori in Ota Ward was nearly twenty kilometers, which seemed like it would take at least that long, but apparently, the GPS's estimated time didn't apply to the Accelerator.

Its lights flashing, the motorcycle zipped from Waseda Avenue to Kagurazaka, then entered the Shuto Expressway at Nishikanda. As they passed the Electronic Toll Collection gate, the motorcycle's siren blared shrilly.

Since today was still the third day of the New Year's holiday, traffic was flowing smoothly, but there were still more than a few cars on the road. Moreover, the Shuto Expressway was structured almost like a circuit, so full of twists and turns that there didn't seem to be a straight section to be found.

Nonetheless, Yumiko unhesitatingly opened up the accelerator and started weaving between the left and right lanes effortlessly. The GPS speed indicator at the bottom left of the display immediately rose past ninety-five kilometers per hour and continued climbing at a frightening speed. Even sitting in the back, Minoru felt like he was about to fly off at any moment, so he could only guess how intense the wind pressure was for Yumiko.

I really can't just stay behind Yumiko forever...

Just as the thought crossed Minoru's mind, Yumiko twisted her right wrist sharply. The three-cylinder engine gave a high-pitched roar; the intense torque pushed the body of the motorcycle forward...

Then Yumiko's ability amplified that speed many times over.

Zoom! The motorcycle seemed to snap the air itself as it took off down the center of the two lanes like a bullet. For just a moment, the digital speedometer read over three hundred kilometers per hour.

As soon as they all but teleported across the short straight section of the Shuto Expressway and the tires touched back down on the ground after floating about five centimeters in the air, sparks flew from the brake rotor and the motorcycle sharply decelerated. They cleared the corner at a bank angle so low Minoru's knee practically scraped the ground, before fiercely accelerating again along the next straight portion of the expressway.

Unlike the previous times, Minoru somehow managed to refrain from screaming, but he couldn't help but seriously consider buying a motorcycle of his own.

When the motorcycle had made it along the Shuto Expressway from the Ikebukuro line to the Yaesu line, then down to the Heiwajima interchange via the Haseda line, the visor display clock showed a time of 7:09 p.m. Just as she had declared, Yumiko had made it across central Tokyo in less than fifteen minutes.

Stopping the siren, they rode farther with only the flashing lights for another two minutes.

The pair dismounted from the motorcycle about ninety meters away from the scene, informed headquarters that they had arrived, and took off their helmets. Yumiko removed her leg warmers as well. She was still wearing her riding shoes, but this looked natural enough, since they matched the jacket she was wearing over her uniform.

Yumiko's helmet and leg warmers went into the rear case along with Minoru's messenger bag, and Minoru's helmet was hooked onto the side. Since it was a full-face helmet, it usually felt rather cramped to wear, but this time he felt a bit uneasy when he removed it.

"Since Stinger aims for the ears, it would be nice if we could keep our helmets on..."

Yumiko shrugged lightly in response.

"That's true enough, but it would look rather unnatural to walk around with helmets on, and it would likely give us away to the enemy all the faster. But don't worry—we can protect our ears with these."

Yumiko reached into the breast pocket of her biker's jacket and produced two pairs of wireless earbuds. Transparent antenna-like parts extended from the metal housing.

"They just completed these prototypes at headquarters, so I brought them along. Try it out."

"A...all right."

Minoru accepted his pair and pushed them into his ears. They fit quite tightly into his ear canals, probably to prevent them from coming out if the wearer moved around too violently, so Minoru could hardly hear any external sound.

But as soon as the power supply turned on automatically, the sounds of his surroundings were audible again. "How is it? Can you hear?" Yumiko was wearing her headphones as well; although her voice was probably being conveyed to him through the wireless communication, it sounded perfectly natural.

"Yes, very clearly... Were these made just because of Stinger?"

"Goodness, of course not. Development on these started long before that. I'll explain their original purpose later—for now, let's just get to the scene."

"Right!"

Nodding to each other, the two began to run along the residential street.

Before long, they saw a number of police cars with their red lights blazing. The narrow road was completely sealed off, with yellow tape stretched across it. The four-story apartment building on the other side seemed to be the scene of the crime.

If this were a comic or a movie, the secret organization agents would probably push through the warning tape and flash their IDs dramatically at the police offers on the scene. Unfortunately, the SFD had no such identity cards. Apparently, only the National Police Agency Security Bureau's and the Public Safety Department of the police headquarters knew of the SFD's existence, so high schoolers like Minoru and Yumiko waving around identity cards wouldn't mean a thing to the policemen present.

Therefore, the pair stopped behind the dozens of onlookers and started by smelling the air.

There was no trace of the particular bestial smell of Ruby Eyes in the chilly night air. If the person who killed the two residents was Stinger, they were long gone.

We'll probably need DD's searching ability to track Stinger from here... As if reading Minoru's thoughts, the voice of the man himself came through the wireless earbuds.

"DD here. Sorry, Yumiko, I got caught in traffic by the Yamate Tunnel... I'm going to change routes at the next exit, but I won't be there until around seven."

The earbuds apparently had some kind of network connection function, making it easy to communicate without taking out their smartphones every time. Minoru imagined appreciatively that this must have been the "original purpose" of the earbuds.

"Understood," Yumiko responded in a low voice. "There are no signs of Ruby Eyes on the scene at the moment. We'll search the surrounding area."

"Roger that. Just be careful, got it?"

Once the conversation ended, the two of them looked at each other.

"...We can't wait another twenty-five minutes."

"Right... I'm worried about the Jet Eye who Stinger might have been targeting. It seems like they escaped from here all right, but we have to help them before Stinger gets them..."

Yumiko nodded.

"Of course... Which way would you run if it was you, Utsugi?"

Surprised by the question, Minoru looked around uncertainly.

The apartment complex was surrounded by other buildings on three sides, so the only escape route was the road where they were standing. So the question was whether they went east or west...

In his mind, Minoru imagined the map of the area he'd formed as they traveled. To the west of here, there was a large residential area with a complicated network of thin, intertwined roads.

To the east, on the other hand, the road continued past the rails and the national highway to an area of reclaimed land. There were no houses at all, only warehouses, factories, parks, wholesale markets, and so on.

"East...I think."

Minoru turned.

"The most frightening thing about Stinger's ability is that you could be shot with a spinebug from the shadows at any moment. I didn't notice anyone was there until one stabbed my neck... So open spaces of reclaimed land would probably be safer than a convoluted residential area."

"Hmm...yes, you're right. Let's go this way, then."

Yumiko started to run as soon as she finished speaking, so Minoru hurried after her.

They passed under the railway track and Route 1 overpass, heading toward the Heiwajima landfill. As they ran, both continued to check the air for signs of the Ruby Eye. The beastly smell would be their best hope of finding the solitary enemy in such a large area.

Even so, a Third Eye holder's ability to sense another generally only worked within a few dozen meters and was only clear if the other person used their own ability. This would be much easier for DD, who had an incomparable sense of smell... But there was nothing they could do about his getting stuck in traffic.

Trying to maximize the use of his nose as best he could, Minoru ran with his face tilted slightly upward.

As a result, though, he was less watchful of the ground below.

Before he knew it, his foot caught in a small depression in the road, sending him swiftly to the ground. He just barely managed to avoid landing face-first by throwing his arms out in front of him but ended up in a position that made it look like he was doing push-ups.

"Hey, are you all right?!"

Yumiko came running back with an expression that was half-concerned and half-exasperated.

"...I'm fine," Minoru mumbled, embarrassed. "I just took my eyes off the ground a little too much..."

"That happens quite often with new Jet Eyes. I'm sure you'll be more careful now that you've fallen once."

Yumiko held out her right hand, and Minoru took it with his left.

But just as she was helping him to his feet—

"......!!"

Minoru's eyes widened, and he let go of Yumiko's hand.

"Ah! Hey!"

The sudden release set Yumiko off-balance, and she toppled onto the ground herself. She looked like she was about to start yelling right there, but Minoru held up a hand to stop her.

"Yumiko...that smell!"

At that, Yumiko's expression changed from anger to confusion. Taking his eyes off her face, Minoru put both hands back on the pavement and concentrated solely on his nose.

He definitely felt something. It was very faint, but there was no mistaking that smell. There was nothing else in the city that would smell so savage and wild.

Searching for the source, Minoru moved to his left, still on all fours. The road toward the landfill had two lanes, so a car could come up from behind at any moment, but Minoru trusted that to Yumiko and closed his eyes. He followed the scent, so sparse that the slightest breeze might blow it away.

After a few dozen seconds, the odor seemed to become a little stronger... Minoru opened his eyes.

There was something lying along the side of the road. An incredibly thin thread, shining faintly in the light of the streetlamps.

Minoru picked it up delicately between his fingertips, and the thread snapped, dangling about twenty centimeters from his fingers.

"Yumiko, look at this."

Yumiko approached dubiously, and Minoru held up the practically weightless string in front of her nose. Yumiko sniffed it cautiously, then drew back sharply as if repulsed.

"......! It smells like a Ruby..."

"Exactly... I think this was made by Stinger's ability. The Professor said the wireworm was made up of thousands of extremely fine threads. This must be one of those..."

"...But why would it be lying by the road? A thread this thin couldn't be used for attacking or defending..."

Yumiko trailed off, suddenly realizing the answer.

"Wait...it must be for tracking!"

"I think so, too. Stinger must have attached a thread-producing insect to the fleeing Jet Eye, to use for chasing them down after killing the witnesses..."

"Which means...the Stinger is on the other end of this thread!"

Yumiko stooped down and looked at the surface of the road. Before long, she looked up and exclaimed to Minoru.

"If it were daytime we probably wouldn't be able to see it, but now the reflecting light makes it just barely visible! Come on!"

"R...right! I'll keep an eye on our surroundings!"

Yumiko began following the thread as she ran, and Minoru followed, casting his eyes around at the road and the buildings nearby.

* * *

In an area with plenty of water, even if he couldn't defeat his opponent, he certainly wouldn't lose.

Ryuu Mikawa, the Trancer, had always been confident in that. But now, he ran right through Heiwanomori Park and Heiwajima Park, where there was a very large pond, and kept running east.

It wasn't that he was so terrified of X, the Ruby-hunting Ruby Eye with the insect-creating ability. It was certainly a difficult ability to deal with, but Mikawa could handle it if he had a large source of water, and it was possible that his water-bottle bomb had rendered the other Ruby incapable of chasing him in the first place.

And yet, the uneasy tension in his stomach hadn't eased up in the slightest.

Perhaps it wasn't because of X so much as the fact that he still didn't know why that person had appeared.

He could just wait for X to catch up, so he could fight the other Ruby Eye and win. But there were other potential problems to worry about.

If the Syndicate, or even Liquidizer herself, had decided to get rid of Mikawa and sent an assassin after him, the situation was very grave. The Syndicate had given Mikawa a name, a home, and living expenses, and now all that would be cut off. More worrying still, even if Mikawa defeated X, sooner or later, there would be another attacker... Liquidizer might even come to wipe Mikawa out herself.

What should I do? No, what do I want to do?

His mind still full of panic and confusion, Mikawa crossed the canal over New Heiwa Bridge and entered Tokai 1-chome. If he kept running, he would come out on the Shuto Expressway Wangan line, then he could cross that to the JR railway yard, then—Ooi Futo.

...Well, that's fine, Mikawa thought unexpectedly.

If the time came for him to die, he would die, and that was that. It was too bad he wouldn't be able to realize his dream of a Snowball Earth, but without the Syndicate...without Liquidizer's help, he would've already been killed by the black hunters by now anyway. Besides, since he'd killed so many innocent people already, it would be laughable for Mikawa to suddenly panic when his turn arrived.

But at the very least, he wanted to choose where he would die. He wanted to enter eternal sleep in that cold and quiet place, together with OO.

Pulling out his smartphone, which he'd been gripping inside his jacket pocket, Mikawa tapped the phone application resolutely.

Since Liquidizer was probably the only person he'd ever call on this phone, it would have made sense to make a shortcut directly to her number on the home screen, but then her information would easily be compromised if the phone fell into enemy hands. Instead, he used a special app that didn't leave a call history and quickly input the number he'd memorized. Of course, it was still possible that someone could access the call records through the carrier company, but at least this would buy them some time in that situation.

Wondering if this phone call would be his last, Mikawa listened to the ringing tone.

After three rings, the other party picked up.

"It's me."

Her voice sounded the same as always. Mikawa gathered strength in his gut and cut to the chase.

"This is Mikawa. I was attacked at my apartment."

There was a sharp gasp on the other line.

"A Jet Eye? Are you hurt, boy?"

He could hear a touch of surprise and worry underneath her cool tone, but if she was acting, Mikawa wouldn't be able to tell. All he could do was relay the facts to her.

"I'm not injured, but I had to use a water-bottle bomb to get away, so it probably caused a big scene. The police may have come by now."

"That hardly matters. Right now, you should just be focused on getting away from the black hunters."

"About that…"

Mikawa recalled the eerie figure of the Ruby Eye in the red coat as he spoke.

"It was a red Third Eye holder that attacked me, not a black one. There's no doubt in my mind—I didn't smell anything even when they used their ability. It's probably the same person who killed the Self-Defense Forces agents at Keihinjima…"

"X?! Why would that person show up at your house…?!"

The shock in Liquidizer's voice definitely sounded genuine to Mikawa as she spoke faster.

"If there was an information leak from the Syndicate, the safe houses will be dangerous, too—you mustn't go near them. I'll pick you up elsewhere. Where are you now?!"

This was the moment of truth.

Mikawa closed his eyes for just a moment as he ran, then spoke.

"I'm heading for the place where you found me last night."

"Understood. We'll meet there, then. I'll be there in thirty…no, twenty-five minutes."

"All right. The enemy could be anywhere by now, so please drive safely."

After ending the call, Mikawa breathed deeply.

If Liquidizer arrived to kill Mikawa instead of save him, he didn't plan on running anymore. He would resist, of course—he would fight back with all his might, with intent to kill equal to hers. But if he lost anyway…he would ask to be allowed to freeze to death in the cold-storage warehouse instead of being liquefied. She seemed like the type of woman who would at least listen to her former pupil's last request, perhaps.

Passing through the vast container yard and crossing the track of the Tokaido freight line, Mikawa entered the warehouse district of Ooi Futo. Because of the holiday, there wasn't a car or person in sight. Mikawa looked back from time to time, but there was no sign that anyone was following him.

Mikawa swerved left as he continued running along the dark road. Around the time that the scent of the tide started to reach him, a familiar square silhouette appeared before his eyes.

An old cold-storage warehouse built some decades ago. He had just been there earlier that day, but it seemed like a completely different place at night—not like a commercial facility that was still in use by any means. At night, it was as desolate as a tomb.

With that uncharacteristic thought, Mikawa crossed the truck yard and headed around to the side of the warehouse.

There were no vehicles in the parking lot, which was overgrown with withered plants. Liquidizer had said she would arrive in twenty-five minutes, but if she was on her way to kill him, she would probably be there earlier. Walking up to the water faucet on the wall of the warehouse, Mikawa opened the tap. Then he breathed on the drainage area to freeze it, so that the water spread out in a black pool over the asphalt.

Mikawa suppressed the desire to enter the cold-storage warehouse with the key in his left pocket. It would technically be easier to fight inside, but he didn't want the pillar that contained OO to be caught in the cross fire from Liquidizer and melt. That was the one thing he refused to allow.

But even outside, he could still hold his own if he had enough water.

Mikawa scooped up some of the ice-cold water gushing out of the tap. Then he breathed carefully on the little pool in his hands. The clump got bigger little by little, until he pulled his hand away when it was about ten centimeters around.

What was left in his palm was a transparent sphere of ice. It had taken no small amount of training until he could use his ability to control the solidification of water enough to make a perfect sphere.

He had eliminated as much of the impurities of the tap water as possible, such as minerals and chlorine, so the resultant ball of ice was hard and wouldn't melt easily. Mikawa continued producing more of the balls, rolling them into various parts of the parking lot as the puddle gradually spread over it. Since the asphalt was a dark black and the ice balls were perfectly transparent, it was hard to distinguish them from the reflected light on the surface of the water, even for Mikawa.

To finish his preparations, he made three more, hiding one in each pocket of his jacket and one in his left hand.

According to the cheap quartz watch on his left wrist, there were still fifteen minutes until Liquidizer's estimated arrival time. She could show up at any moment. There were two entrances to the parking lot, one through the truck yard in front and a general entrance gate at the back; Liquidizer would probably use the back entrance. Mikawa stood in the center of the puddle and turned to face that way. The cold water soaked into his sneakers, but he paid no attention.

Despite the tense situation, Mikawa's mind was strangely calm.

A plane passed almost frighteningly low on its way to land at Haneda Airport, using the new route that began operation last year to coincide with the Tokyo Olympics. The loud roar did nothing to disturb Mikawa's mental state, but it did wipe out all other sounds around him for an instant.

So this time, it was because Mikawa was concentrating all his senses that he noticed it, not mere coincidence.

Mixed in with the roar of the airplane...an incredibly tiny sound of wind behind his head.

"......!"

Mikawa ducked instinctively, and a flying object skimmed over his neck at high speed. It felt exactly the same as when he was attacked at the entrance to his apartment.

As the object whipped past, then turned back toward him sharply, Mikawa kicked the water at his feet toward it with all his might. Then he sent a sharp but quiet breath toward the spray of water. Instead of freezing, the drops of water were supercooled and froze over the flying object as they made contact with it, finally closing it in a thick casing of ice.

The lump of ice dropped into the puddle at Mikawa's feet with a splash, and he crushed it under his sneaker before quickly turning around.

At the entrance of the parking lot, near the edge of the truck yard, lurked a single silhouette.

The light of a distant streetlight revealed a long dark-red coat with a matte texture. The person's gloves were the same color, and they wore long boots on their feet. And once again, the large hood masked their face in total darkness.

Mikawa smelled the air once again.

Just as he'd expected, there was no trace of the chemical odor black abilities gave off.

There was no doubt about it. This was the red-coated Ruby Eye who had attacked him at home.

But how had the enemy found him here when he was so sure he'd shaken off any tails?

The answer was obvious. Mikawa's brain refused to accept it for a while, but he couldn't deny the facts right before his eyes.

Liquidizer must have sent that Ruby hunter after him. Immediately after the call from Mikawa, she had contacted and sent X to this place. He could think of no other explanation.

In other words, Mikawa had been cast aside—by the Syndicate executive, his mentor, his former master who'd treated him to *okonomiyaki*.

Mikawa was a little surprised by how much shock and despair he felt. Because they were both homicidal Ruby Eyes, he had always known this time would come, and he'd been fully prepared to try to kill her earlier that evening if she tried to melt OO's ice...or so he had thought.

And yet.

If he couldn't avoid fighting, he would have preferred his opponent to be his master herself. Mikawa had no intention of being erased like a simple task by a Ruby Eye whose name and face he didn't even know.

This was the second time he had dodged X's attack, which should have been a certain kill if this was an assassination attempt, yet the enemy showed no signs of being shaken. The Ruby Eye's long boots splashed into the puddle in which Mikawa stood as they unhesitatingly crossed the parking lot toward him.

If this person was working for Liquidizer, surely she would have revealed Mikawa's ability; since they weren't avoiding the water, they were either incredibly confident in their own ability or simply reckless. In any case, if Mikawa was going to fight, he had no intention of holding back.

Mikawa switched the ice ball in his left hand over to his right, then hurled it at the enemy's left side.

The distance between them was about twenty-four meters. This was farther than it had been back in front of Mikawa's home, but the ice ball was much faster and easier to control than the water bottle.

Just as Mikawa had planned, the other Ruby tried to move to the right to avoid the ball.

In that direction, another ice ball that Mikawa had rolled was lying in wait. Concentrating on both of them at once, Mikawa breathed a long, wide breath.

He didn't simply melt the ice balls. Instead, he left an outer shell of less than a centimeter of ice and heated the interior into steam in an instant.

The thought that Mikawa released with full power—the invisible energy that the Syndicate apparently called the seventh force—violently shook the water molecules inside the ice, turning them to high-pressure, high-temperature steam.

The huge amount of pressure was too much for the brittle outer shell of the ice ball, and it held for only a fraction of an instant before exploding with a high-pitched *boom*.

The ice shell shattered into countless sharp fragments, flying into the red-coated attacker from the left and right. The rest of the ice bullets mostly shot up toward the sky, but a few hit the side of the warehouse, and some even flew toward Mikawa. He turned them back to water with a quick breath, catching them on his jacket.

This ice grenade had pierced even the special battle suits of the high-tech SFD, causing serious injury to Divider, so no ordinary store-bought coat could possibly defend against it. The other Ruby had likely taken a lot of damage.

However, his mentor had taught him not to let his guard down at times like these. Even if the enemy went down, you had to keep attacking without mercy until the Third Eye left their bodies. Until then, there was no assuming that you'd won.

Huffff...

Mikawa sent a sharp breath toward the puddle at the staggering X's feet. The puddle, which was nearly five centimeters deep, froze over a two-meter radius, trapping the enemy's feet. The Ruby Eye wouldn't be able to move now without removing their boots.

Mikawa took out another ice ball from his right pocket and took aim.

This time, he would toss it right into the hood that hid the Ruby's face.

If an ice grenade exploded right in front of someone's face, the shards would pierce the skull and dig right into the brain. No human being could survive that, not even a Ruby or a Jet.

Mikawa started to throw with all his might, but as he did so, his eyes widened for just an instant.

Glittering in the distant streetlight, countless fragments of ice were crumbling away from X's entire body. Those were the ice bullets that had dug into the fabric of the coat. It looked as if not a single one had gotten through.

Mikawa was shocked, but he didn't let it break his posture. Instead, he instantly moved his aim lower.

Liquidizer had instructed him to refine his strongest weapons to the maximum limit, so he had practiced his pitching in the numerous parks in the nearby area of reclaimed land. A man who was apparently the coach of a local sandlot baseball team even told him that he was good enough to make the team.

There was no way X could dodge Mikawa's low fastball, even by ducking. It wouldn't be as dangerous as a direct hit to the face, but if Mikawa blew up the ice grenade just as it hit somewhere on his opponent's body, he should still be able to land a fatal wound.

The ice ball whistled as it flew through the air.

Then, the red-coated Ruby Eye effortlessly slipped both boots out of the ice frozen around them, stepping to the right to avoid it.

Dumbfounded, Mikawa heard the ice ball crash into something in the darkness of the truck yard and smash to pieces.

Why was X able to move? Long boots or not, they shouldn't have been able to pull out from five-centimeter-thick ice so easily.

Had they predicted that the boots might get frozen and coated the slick surface in oil or something?

If so, then surely that was at Liquidizer's instruction. His former master was using the utmost care to ensure that she killed Mikawa...no, that this mysterious Ruby Eye X could kill him.

As a fresh wave of realization went through his mind, Mikawa lost his strength for just a moment.

And as if aiming for that very instant—

X raised their left hand, and three small objects were launched out of the palm in rapid succession.

The insects. I have to stop them. Some part of Mikawa's brain, or maybe it was his Ruby Eye itself, made him move half automatically to kick up the water at his feet.

He breathed on the wall of splashing water to supercool it. That would stop the insect attacks. Then he would make all of the remaining ice balls in the puddle explode...

But then—

The three insects, moving at a speed just barely visible even to a Ruby Eye's vision, spouted white flames from their back ends.

Accelerating like tiny missiles, the bugs shook off Mikawa's kinetic vision and disappeared. The beads of supercooled water were smashed in midair, turning into a fine spray.

Immediately after, Mikawa felt a sharp impact and burning heat in his right shoulder, left arm, and the middle of his abdomen. As he fell backward into the puddle, he knew that the three needlelike insects had pierced him.

Intense pain set in two seconds later, but Mikawa fought it off as he assessed the damage.

The wounds in his shoulder and arm were painful but certainly not life-threatening. However, the abdominal wound was a bad one. It felt like his vital organs had taken damage, and the sword wound on his chest had started bleeding again from impact of the fall.

He had to activate the rest of the grenades and fast.

Covering the wound in his right shoulder with his left hand, Mikawa managed to raise himself up with just his right hand.

Then he saw another white light.

A fourth missile insect pierced through the right side of his chest and exited through his back. Mikawa fell back to the ground.

The grenades...

Still determined, Mikawa tried to breathe toward the remaining ice balls while still lying in the puddle.

But the air wouldn't enter his chest. A hole in one of his lungs was causing an open pneumothorax. His right lung had collapsed enough to cease functioning. The left lung was somehow still functioning, but his wounds from Divider prevented him from breathing in enough air.

As a result, Mikawa could no longer activate his abilities as the Trancer.

The Ruby Eye X walked soundlessly toward the fallen Mikawa.

As usual, he couldn't see the face underneath the hood. He couldn't feel any emotions, either.

Who was it who said that Third Eye holders' abilities all came, without exception, from a fear of the world around them? Mikawa had empathized with those words. It was certainly more than likely that the wall Mikawa had felt between himself and others since a young age was created by fear. The day that he learned that OO would never wake up again only crystallized that. Mikawa hated the world that had refused to save OO, and somewhere deep in his heart, he grew fearful of the most common substance in the world, water.

Human beings are made of water. When he thought about that, Mikawa was seized with a deep fear.

However, this X showed no signs of any such fear. The source of the ability to produce and control insects should theoretically be a fear of insects, but X's behavior was too indifferent...as if their ability was nothing more than a tool.

"...Are...you...?"

Mikawa coughed up bloody foam as he tried to speak in a muffled voice.

Are you really a Ruby Eye? he wanted to ask, but his voice refused to come out.

Reaching a distance of about nine meters away, the other Ruby Eye lifted their left hand. The nozzle-like metal circle in the center of the gloved palm produced a new insect with a faint sound.

This wasn't one of the elongated missile insects but the round thorn type that had originally attacked Mikawa. If it entered his body, there would be no recovering. He couldn't defend himself, so he had to evade it somehow.

Yet, in spite of this knowledge, his body wouldn't move. His body was rapidly losing oxygen because of his inability to breathe sufficiently.

With a faint whizzing sound, the thorn insect drew a large arc in the air and swooped toward Mikawa's neck.

But just then—

Someone burst into the parking lot through the thick shrubbery on the left side. Flinging their body forward, the newcomer stretched out their right hand and caught the insect that was about to pierce Mikawa's neck. Immediately afterward, a small amount of liquid splashed to the ground.

...Master...? Why would you save me...?

His head foggy from lack of oxygen, Mikawa looked up at his rescuer, who was inspecting the crushed remains of the insect with an expression of faint surprise. Then, forgetting for a moment that he was on the verge of death, he gasped.

"...?!"

It wasn't Liquidizer.

It was a boy...around his age, probably a high school student. There was nothing unusual about his jeans and mountain parka, but his unique hair that looked almost silver when light hit it was unmistakable.

It was a Jet Eye. A member of the SFD, code name Isolator.

What are you doing here? Why are you protecting me...?

Without responding to the questions Mikawa couldn't quite voice, the ashen-haired boy quickly picked himself up.

"Run! As far away as you can...!"

The voice, probably directed at Mikawa, had a slightly unnatural ring to it. At that moment, Mikawa realized that Isolator's sneakers weren't touching the water on the ground. He was using his ability, the invisible barrier. The voice seemed to be coming out of a small device fixed to his left wrist from above the force field.

That answered a more minor question, though the mystery as to why a Jet Eye would help Mikawa remained. However, the Isolator scarcely glanced at Mikawa's face as he stood to face off against the red-coated Ruby Eye.

Raising their left hand, X fired a missile insect.

Shooting white flames from its back end, the pointed end of the insect zoomed toward the boy's face—and was knocked away with a dull crack.

As always, the power of that force field was frightfully impressive. X retreated for the first time, trying to get some distance from the Isolator.

The Ruby stopped just outside the puddle Mikawa had made, and then—

Again, from the shrubbery on the left, there was an orange light and three explosive sounds.

A handgun. Again, Mikawa wondered if it was Liquidizer, but again, he was mistaken.

Instead, out leaped a high school girl wearing a leather biker's jacket over her blazer-type uniform, black tights, and riding shoes. It was the Jet Eye who'd been partnered with Isolator before, the Accelerator.

X's body wobbled as the three shots landed.

Mikawa's ice grenade probably had more energy in a single shot, but the bullets likely had better penetration. This time, surely the attack would break through the coat and deal a fatal wound. Ruby Eyes had such inferior equipment to their black counterparts; there was no way they could obtain fully bulletproof clothes...

"...Wha......?"

Once again, his surprise surpassed his fear of imminent death.

The surface of X's red coat moved in several places, as if it were made of living tissue.

It was a repulsive movement, like innumerable earthworms crawling around in the dirt. When the worms withdrew from the three areas they'd converged on, three objects fell away. Mikawa had no doubt that they were the crushed remains of the bullets.

Not only could it resist Mikawa's ice grenade—it could even stand up to real bullets.

This was no ordinary coat. In fact, it wasn't real clothing at all.

The dark-red coat and hood, and possibly even the gloves and boots, were made of the insects that X's power created.

Even if the bullets hadn't pierced, they still should have had an impact similar to being hit by a blunt weapon; yet, X coolly straightened up and pointed their left hand at Accelerator, who looked understandably shocked.

There was a faint shooting sound. This time, it was a thorn insect, not the missile type.

"Yu... Accelerator!"

When the ashen-haired boy cried out, the blazer-clad girl kicked off the ground.

Zoom! The air trembled, and the girl disappeared from sight. It was her ability, acceleration.

The girl reappeared with a huge splash of water not far from Mikawa. She had covered a distance of over eighteen meters in under a second.

However, X's thorn insect was homing in on her. It swerved around in midair, still chasing the Accelerator.

With a large jump, Isolator once again caught it in his hand. Even with his defensive barrier, the boy's courage in unhesitatingly grabbing the insect and his ability to read its flight trajectory was still impressive. Unless…this wasn't his first time fighting X…?

Though his thoughts kept moving, Mikawa could tell that his vision was gradually getting dark.

Even in top condition, Third Eye holders consumed a lot of oxygen in battle. So if their breathing was obstructed, they could easily faint or even die. This was the reason that the Syndicate had been so insistent about recruiting Igniter, who had the ability to control oxygen, and that the SFD had so much trouble fighting him.

Before he died, Mikawa thought, he at least wanted to know why the two Jet Eyes had tried to protect him.

Once he'd crushed the second insect, Isolator shouted through the speaker. Mikawa noticed a small earbud that flashed white only when he was speaking.

"I'll take care of Stinger! Accelerator, get that person out of here!"

Apparently, the SFD had given X the code name Stinger. As usual, they completely lacked subtlety…Mikawa mused to himself as his eyelids grew heavier.

"Understood. Watch out for those worms!"

With that, Accelerator did another short dash to arrive directly next to Mikawa, peering into his face.

Her pretty, if rather tense, face looked suspicious for a moment, then turned guarded and hostile.

"You…you're Trancer!!"

She pointed her gun at Mikawa's chest with both hands.

"What…?!"

Facing off against Stinger, formerly known as X, the Isolator also gave a surprised exclamation.

"…Oh, come on…," Mikawa muttered with what little air was left in his lungs.

Apparently, they hadn't realized that the person lying on the ground was Ryuu Mikawa—the Ruby Eye known as Trancer.

Most likely, they'd assumed that the explosion at Mikawa's apartment was caused by a battle between a Ruby and a Jet and had rushed to the aid of what they assumed was one of their own kind.

In other words, they hadn't been trying to help Mikawa at all—it was just a huge misunderstanding on both sides.

Unexpectedly, a little shaking motion welled up from his broken chest.

At first, he thought his lungs were spasming, but it was something else.

"...Ha-ha..."

What spilled from Mikawa's lips was a weak peal of laughter.

"Wh-why would Ruby Eyes fight one another?!"

Accelerator didn't seem to notice Mikawa's laughter. Her expression hardened, and she moved her index finger back to the trigger.

"...No, it doesn't matter. We'll just have to take care of you, too."

Mikawa didn't know much about guns, but he at least knew that the caliber of a compact automatic pistol was generally nine millimeters. If he was shot with one from such a short distance, that would certainly be enough to kill him.

Whenever possible, the SFD generally preferred to capture Ruby Eyes, render them powerless, and remove the Third Eye with surgery.

But this benevolence didn't extend to Syndicate Ruby Eyes who had killed countless people. Moreover, they were outside, so the Third Eye's exodus wouldn't cause any major destruction.

Mikawa would have preferred to die in the cold-storage warehouse, to freeze to death next to OO... But it didn't look like that was going to happen.

But at least OO was safe in the warehouse just a meter away. Surely, he would at least be able to feel her presence at the moment of his death.

Accelerator's finger began to pull the trigger.

Mikawa closed his eyes and waited.

"Stop!!"

It was then that he heard a strained voice cry out from nearby.

Accelerator moved in a flash. Somehow managing to lift his heavy eyelids, Mikawa saw that the schoolgirl in the leather jacket was now pointing her gun somewhere at the back of the parking lot.

Mikawa couldn't look, as he didn't have enough power left to move his head. But he recognized the voice as belonging to his former master—Liquidizer.

"Stop. Don't shoot the child."

Her voice cracked a little as she spoke.

Master, why do you sound so desperate? Mikawa asked in the back of his mind.

Wasn't Liquidizer the one who'd sent Stinger to this warehouse? He still didn't know why, but it was probably an order from the Syndicate top brass, or else Mikawa had become a hindrance to her personally. Guessing this, Mikawa had forced himself to accept the shock and sorrow of being tossed aside by his former master—so why was she saying such things to the black hunters now? And in such a pleading voice, no less.

No...there was another mystery here, too.

If Liquidizer was the one who told Stinger that Mikawa was here at the warehouse, how had the two Jet Eyes gotten here? There was no way they could have caught up to him from the scene of the explosion in Oomori...

But of course, Mikawa had no strength left to voice these questions.

"...Liquidizer...," Accelerator murmured in a stunned voice, then turned the gun back toward Mikawa.

She knew from their fight three days ago that Liquidizer could liquefy bullets easily.

Instead, the girl pointed the gun straight at Mikawa's heart and spoke.

∗ ∗ ∗

"...Liquidizer..."

Minoru heard Yumiko's voice behind him via the earbuds he was wearing.

As it turned out, the real "intended purpose" of these high-tech wireless earpieces made by the SFD was for communication through Minoru's protective shell. The sapphire glass antenna extending from the housing had a built-in LED transmitter and photodiode receiver for visible light communication.

Minoru's shell deflected all elementary particles and electromagnetic waves, except for visible light. This device utilized that characteristic to convert voices into optical signals and transmit them from the LED on the end of the antenna. The photodiodes in Yumiko's earbuds decoded that and reproduced the data as sound. Of course, the reverse was possible as well.

They had used an optical transmitter functioning on the same principle when Minoru entered the reactor core in the Tokyo Bay Nuclear Power Plant, but this version was much more flexible. Now one of the biggest issues with Minoru's protective shell, the fact that it blocked all sound, had been resolved thanks to this technology.

In addition, Minoru's earbuds could also communicate with a high-performance mic and speaker system attached on top of his protective shell with a plastic band, which could reproduce Minoru's voice and pick up the sounds of his surroundings.

The only disadvantages were that since the communication used visible light, the earbuds shone when he spoke, and if there was an obstacle between them, he couldn't communicate at all—but apparently, they might eventually be able to resolve those issues, too.

At any rate, thanks to these earbuds, Minoru was able to hear Yumiko's voice. But he couldn't help but be shocked by what she was actually saying.

The victim they'd traced by following the extremely narrow thread, expecting to rescue a new Jet Eye…was actually Olivier Saito's archenemy, Trancer, who they'd fought in Minami-Aoyama just three days ago.

And now, apparently, the incredibly powerful Liquidizer had even shown up to save him.

If all that were true, it made the situation even more confusing. The target whom the red-coated Ruby Eye assassin, Stinger, had assaulted at the apartment in Oomori West and chased down using those threads… was a fellow Ruby Eye?

Now Stinger's actions made less sense than ever.

Three days ago, on New Year's Eve, the Ruby used spinebugs to kill six elite STS members when they broke into a Syndicate hideout at Keihinjima.

Earlier today, Stinger killed two ordinary people at the NCAM hospital in Shinjuku, hid there for six hours, and attacked Minoru when he came to visit Olivier, running away without killing him.

And just three hours later, there was the attack on the Ruby Eye Trancer in Oomori West, Ota Ward. Trancer had escaped the first time, but Stinger chased him down to this warehouse.

The Ruby Eye's targets and actions were simply too inconsistent.

The six Special Task Squad members were ordinary people without Third Eyes, Minoru was a Jet Eye, and Trancer was a Ruby Eye. Keihinjima was a Syndicate hideout, while NCAM in Toyama was an SFD-affiliated hospital.

On top of that, nobody knew how Stinger had gotten information about both the Keihinjima warehouse and NCAM.

The only clear fact was that Stinger was an incredibly dangerous Ruby Eye. And now there were two new powers to worry about—in addition to the spinebugs and wireworms, they had now seen Stinger produce high-speed missile-like insects that shot around with flames and the living "coat" that could shift around and deflect nine-millimeter bullets. And there was no guarantee that this was the end of it.

They had to stop Stinger here and now, no matter what, before any more innocent victims were killed.

But now Minoru didn't dare move. Because behind him, Yumiko was facing off with Liquidizer.

"And what makes you think I would listen to a request like that, Liquidizer?"

Yumiko's voice sounded as if she was fighting to suppress her emotions.

"Trancer here has killed more than ten innocent people. If I don't eliminate him while I have the chance, I might as well give up being a Jet Eye. I never would have helped him if I knew who he was—I could have just stayed hidden and watched while Stinger killed him."

Minoru couldn't tell if that was what Yumiko really would have done, but he understood that it was the most logical choice.

After a moment, Liquidizer's voice reached Minoru's ears, picked up by Yumiko's earbuds and amplified automatically.

"Nevertheless, I ought to thank you for saving the boy's life."

"Don't mock me!!" Yumiko snapped furiously. "I didn't mean to help him! I'm going to get rid of him right now!!"

There was a faint metallic *click*—Yumiko had probably raised the hammer of the SIG P224.

"Stop that at once! If you kill that child now, you'll just become another chess piece manipulated by your whims!"

"You have no right to say that when you people have killed so many on your own whims!"

Yumiko's voice was rising in anger.

"I'm begging you, stop!" Liquidizer pleaded.

"Well, this just won't do…"

A voice murmured.

Minoru couldn't tell right away where it had come from, since it was intermingled with Liquidizer's cry in the optical communicator.

Just then, Stinger, who'd been standing still, suddenly moved.

The Ruby's left hand raised quickly, aiming at someone behind Minoru. Instinctively, Minoru moved too, blocking the shot. Whether it was a spinebug or a missilebug, he absolutely had to block it.

The faint shooting sound produced a spinebug this time. It seemed to be aimed somewhere far to the right of Yumiko's position, but this bug could freely alter its path at any moment.

"I won't let you…!"

Shouting inside his shell, Minoru leaped to the right, stretching out his right hand and grabbing the bug out of the air. Since he'd watched their trajectories at NCAM and here at the warehouse, he knew by now that the spinebugs couldn't make very sharp turns. With Third Eye–enhanced vision, it wasn't impossible to catch them mid-flight.

Still, Minoru felt like it was nothing short of miraculous that he had succeeded three times in a row as he crushed the spinebug through his protective shell.

The insect broke with a snap, letting loose a spray of viscous, semi-transparent liquid. Since the surface of the shell was frictionless, the liquid fell with the remains of the insect when he opened his hand and disappeared into the puddle at his feet.

Just as when he'd crushed the first two insects, a faint sense of unease swept through his mind.

The Professor had said the spinebugs' abdomens contained a high-powered explosive called acetone peroxide. He'd seen it in action when one of the bugs was hit into a pillar by Olivier's sword and exploded.

Because of that, Minoru had assumed that the insects would explode when he crushed them. However, all that actually happened was that they released a small amount of liquid.

Was the pressure of crushing it with a hand not enough to cause an explosion? Was there some special condition necessary? Or perhaps...

But he didn't have a chance to continue down this line of thought.

As Minoru landed with one knee on the ground from his horizontal jump—

The Stinger's red coat began to squirm in several places, like when it had caught the bullets before, and swelled outward.

Lumps formed like giant warts, then fired dozens of thin threads at the same time.

Wireworms!

The cords spread out radially, five or six of them clearly moving toward Minoru. He tried to avoid them, but he'd been caught in the moment he broke his readied stance to crush the spinebug, so his reaction was just a second too late. Above the shell, two wireworms wrapped around his upper body and one below his knee, instantly forming loops around Minoru to restrain him.

"Damn...!"

Minoru gritted his teeth and yanked at the strands around his legs with both hands, but the incredibly thin wire was as unbending as it had been at the hospital. According to the Professor, it would be impossible to break the wire with brute strength, since it was made up of thousands of microscopic polymer fibers twisted together.

Losing his balance and falling to the ground, Minoru twisted around to check on Yumiko.

Although pointing the gun at Trancer should have slowed her down, Yumiko had accelerated a short distance away to avoid two of the wireworms. However, there were simply too many insects attacking. Flying at her just above the ground, a third wireworm caught her by the legs and sent her tumbling to the ground. More of the bugs swarmed over her, wrapping around her entire body several times over.

Since Liquidizer was farthest away from Stinger, she would probably be able to fend off any insects and escape the battlefield.

However, when Minoru finally spotted her, she was still standing at the edge of the parking lot, ready to take on the wireworms that flew at her from all directions.

Her hands flew around with fingers outstretched, so quickly they seemed to leave afterimages in the air. Each time they made contact with a worm, it scattered into droplets of reddish-brown liquid.

Instead of the business suit she'd been wearing when Minoru first encountered her at the Minami-Aoyama Syndicate base, she was wearing a navy-blue school uniform and thick black glasses. Dark-red stains spread over her pure-white ascot tie, but she didn't seem concerned as her hands flew through the air as if she were dancing.

Liquefying all twenty or so wireworms easily, Liquidizer launched herself forward, her black loafers kicking off the stain she'd created on the asphalt.

Weaving through the gap between the fallen Yumiko and Trancer, Liquidizer's pleated skirt fluttered as she dashed at top speed. The puddle at her feet barely made a splash as she sprinted, as if she were gliding over the water's surface.

Without so much as a glance at Minoru, she passed right in front of him to charge at Stinger.

The insect user nonchalantly raised their left hand and fired a missilebug.

The bug flew forward at super-high speed, and Liquidizer deflected it with superhuman reflexes. The sharp-tipped bug was liquefied in an instant, but the propulsion agent—probably a similar substance to the spinebug's liquid—caused a small explosion, drawing a spray of blood from Liquidizer's left hand.

But the woman didn't slow down. Taking a long step forward with her right leg, she pushed her right hand against the center of Stinger's chest.

It's over, Minoru thought. Liquidizer's hand could liquefy anything it touched, whether it was resin, metal, or even a human body.

Stinger's coat undulated in concentric circles, turning into a dark-red liquid.

But then, instantly, the liquid changed into countless threadlike insects—wireworms.

The worms entwined around one another, fusing together and reforming the coat almost at once. Surprise registered across Liquidizer's face for just a moment, and she once again pushed her right hand forward.

The same phenomenon repeated itself. That was all.

Immediately afterward, Stinger moved.

Without any preliminary motion, as if unaffected by gravity or human physiology, Stinger's right leg shot out at an unbelievable speed, landing a kick square in Liquidizer's abdomen.

"Ngh…"

Liquidizer's slim frame was thrown into the air. Then, with an even more unnatural movement, Stinger's right leg followed up with such rapid kicks that the right foot seemed to vanish from sight.

Even through the mic on his left wrist, Minoru could clearly hear a bone crack in Liquidizer's left arm when she tried to use it to protect herself. Her black-rimmed glasses were blown off, shining faintly in the streetlight.

Splashing down in the puddle, Liquidizer's body bounced violently across the pavement and rolled to a halt near Minoru's feet.

Minoru tried to guess at what had happened.

True to her name, Liquidizer could liquefy any solids. However, that also meant that she had no power over substances that were already liquid.

Stinger's coat had certainly liquefied when Liquidizer touched it. But it regenerated at an incredibly high speed before gravity could pull it down, preventing Liquidizer's palm from touching Stinger's actual body.

Yes, it regenerated.

Stinger's fourth power wasn't just the ability to manipulate the red coat like an insect.

The coat itself was made of insects. Countless wireworms fused together to create living clothing. That was why it was able to block bullets just by bulking up the area of impact, launch countless worms from the coat, and even regenerate the liquefied worms.

The power of the Ruby Eye who the Professor had nicknamed "Stinger" was more than just manipulating insects. It was the ability to control the very existence of these artificial creatures—essentially manipulating life.

Lowering their right leg, which was of course covered in a dark-red stocking-like material, Stinger began to walk toward the fallen Liquidizer.

The long boots of the same color splashed quietly as the Ruby walked through the puddle. Liquidizer tried to rise, but the kicks must have injured her internal organs; she coughed up a bit of blood and fell again. Her navy-blue sailor suit turned black as it absorbed water.

Liquidizer and Stinger. Both were Ruby Eyes, enemies of the SFD... enemies of humanity.

This situation, where they were trying to kill each other, was so unexpected that Minoru didn't know how to respond.

If he simply continued to watch, Stinger would kill Liquidizer in a matter of seconds. This was the same woman who had trapped Minoru and Suu Komura in concrete in Minami-Aoyama: the reason that Suu had taken nearly fatal wounds. And in the battle at the factory afterward, she had shown no mercy in trying to kill Minoru and Yumiko.

There was no reason for Minoru to help this person. Just as Yumiko had said earlier, it would be easiest to let Stinger kill Liquidizer and Trancer, then face the remaining Ruby Eye on their own.

And yet...

And yet.

Stricken by an impulse even he didn't understand, Minoru once again tried to break through the three wireworms.

That was when it happened.

Behind the approaching Stinger, something exploded with a loud *boom*.

Mingled with the spray of water, countless tiny white objects flew through the air. Quite a few of them hit the Stinger's back, sending the insect user reeling.

Minoru realized instantly that this was Trancer's ability. He had hidden the same ice grenades that had put Olivier Saito in the hospital throughout the puddle, and now they had exploded. Trancer, whose body was riddled with holes from the missilebugs, must have used the last of his strength to set them off in an attempt to protect Liquidizer.

But Stinger, who was able to withstand even gunshots, didn't so much as fall down from the direct impact of the ice bombs. Though it did send the Ruby stumbling a bit, Stinger recovered quickly, and the face hidden in the hood turned toward the back of the parking lot.

"...We'll start with you, then."

Again, Minoru heard an unfamiliar voice through the earpiece. The optical communication certainly solved the protective shell's biggest issue, but it was still difficult to determine the source of voices and sounds. But Minoru had a feeling that the source of this voice was hidden in the darkness of the red hood.

That face had now turned from Liquidizer toward Trancer. Stinger stepped through the puddle, crossing directly in front of Minoru.

The figure's right hand moved, pulling something out of a coat pocket.

It was a large syringe, nearly twenty centimeters in length.

The moment he saw it, Minoru remembered something from the scene back at the hospital.

When he was stabbed in the neck by a spinebug and pretended to be unconscious, Stinger had been holding the same object while approaching the fallen Minoru. An empty syringe, with the piston fully pushed in.

Professor Riri Isa had said Stinger was the type who wasn't particular about their targets or their methods. Now, Minoru finally realized the source of the discomfort he'd felt at that time.

Certainly, Stinger's insects were designed with the sole purpose of killing or immobilizing enemies. There wasn't anything that seemed to indicate a particular obsession or finesse.

But the syringe was different. Its extremely thin needle was hardly designed to kill, and the syringe itself was empty.

That syringe...that was the real representation of Stinger's inner thoughts. A tool directly connected to the trauma that served as the source of all Third Eye holders' abilities.

Holding the syringe, Stinger probably became the type of killer who chose targets and methods very carefully.

The insect user drew steadily closer to Trancer, who didn't so much as twitch. The glass syringe gleamed in the faint light.

Suddenly, Minoru heard a weak voice.

"...Isolator. I'll take care of those ropes. So please...save him."

The source of the voice was obviously Liquidizer, who was lying just a meter away. Even so, Minoru widened his eyes, unable to believe that the most dangerous and ruthless Ruby Eye was saying such a thing—begging even.

"...Why? He's one of yours."

Her glasses gone, Liquidizer looked at Minoru with eyes that had once reminded him of a polished mirror.

"Who can say...? Until three days ago, he was just a convenient pawn...or so I thought. But now I'm not so sure."

"How did that happen? What could have changed in just three days?"

"…You said something to me that day, boy. That if I have no one I want to protect with my power, I'm much more isolated than you."

Minoru remembered those words, too, though he probably hadn't been thinking logically when he said it. In that desperate situation, his rage, grief, and misery had reached the breaking point and burst out in the form of those words…at least, that was how it seemed to him now.

But even if that was the case, it was still how Minoru genuinely felt.

And it seemed to him that what Liquidizer was saying now wasn't a lie, either.

"…Quite truthfully, that day, I had every intention of abandoning Trancer and escaping alone if I thought I was in danger. I even plotted to kill him if I had to, in order to prevent him from leaking information. But…in the end, I couldn't do it. That was when I realized that I had something I wanted to protect, too."

"…But why him? What makes him so special to you?"

"I don't know. But…perhaps I've always felt some sympathy toward him. That boy has managed to stay himself all this time by hanging on to an illusion. And it's probably his Third Eye that's showing him that illusion. That tiny little sphere is manipulating every one of us, without even realizing it…"

Just as Liquidizer trailed off, the Stinger stopped moving.

Looking down at Trancer, who seemed to have lost consciousness, Stinger nudged him with the toe of a boot a few times. After a moment, the insect user crouched down to peer into his face.

A short distance away, Yumiko was struggling against the wireworms that bound her, trying to reach the gun she'd dropped nearby. However, her arms were completely wrapped up, so she couldn't make it.

Most likely, the Stinger was trying to gather the blood of Third Eye users. Ruby Eye or Jet Eye—it didn't seem to matter. After Trancer, Yumiko was sure to be the next target.

"…I'm not doing it to help Trancer."

Shaking off his conflicted feelings, Minoru spoke.

"It's to help my own…to help Accelerator. If that's good enough for you…then I'll accept your proposal."

"…Thank you."

Liquidizer's lips were wet with fresh blood as she whispered. Then she

reached out with her left hand, which had been badly burned by the missilebugs. One by one, she touched the three wireworms that bound Minoru.

The powerful fibers that made up the bugs were liquefied instantly, and the moment they burst away from his body due to the tension, Minoru stood up quickly.

Stinger's back was still facing Minoru. Victory would depend on whether he could close the approximately eighteen-meter distance between them without being noticed. But the majority of that distance was through the deep puddle.

He couldn't splash through the water. Instead of running on the ground, he had to run on the water's surface.

Minoru stepped forward with his right foot, forming a tiny ripple in the black water.

Go!

Shouting in his mind, Minoru ran forward.

The only noise he heard from the microphone was the faint sound of wind. Even when he stepped with all his might, the surface of the water didn't break, only leaving successive ripples as footprints. Rather than the ground or the water, Minoru seemed to be running on the air itself.

Nine meters…five meters…

When there were only three meters left between them, Stinger, who was about to stab the syringe into Trancer's chest, snapped upright.

With frightening reaction speed, a wireworm shot out from the Stinger's left hand toward Minoru.

But just before it fired, Yumiko suddenly burst onto the scene as if sliding across the ground, slamming herself into Stinger's right leg. Most likely, she had shifted her still-restrained body toward them and used her ability on the modest kinetic energy this created to propel herself forward.

The wireworm that shot out of Stinger's hand missed its target by a long shot, flying harmlessly out of the parking lot.

In the next moment, Minoru spread his arms wide and tackled Stinger, firmly holding the Ruby Eye down.

The insect user was right before his eyes. Yet, even at this short distance, the inside of the hood was still filled with darkness, and all that could be seen were two eyes.

To be more precise, what Minoru saw was the whites of the two eyes that seemed to be floating in a dark-gray void. The pupils were perfectly black, so dark they seemed to suck in all the light around them. They revealed even less of the owner's inner thoughts than Liquidizer's mirror-esque eyes, as if there was only absolute nothingness—

The eyes blinked only once.

Minoru's arms were pushed away, and he gritted his teeth.

Stinger was incredibly powerful. Though the insect user was physically thinner than Minoru, he could tell his opponent was much stronger. At this rate, he would barely last five seconds more.

I have no choice.

Gathering his resolve, Minoru breathed in deeply.

If he did this, it would definitely kill Stinger. But if he didn't, Trancer, Liquidizer, and even Yumiko would be killed, leaving Minoru as the only survivor. He absolutely couldn't allow that. No matter what.

The sphere buried in the center of his chest pulsed.

Energy overflowed from the Third Eye, filling up the interior of the shell with a bright golden glow.

He was going to cause the protective shell to burst with the enemy grasped tightly in his arms. The diffusing shell was strong enough to burst through concrete or metal in an instant. Stinger's body would be completely broken—destroyed beyond any chance of restoring its original shape.

But he still had to do it.

"Aaaaargh!"

With a powerful yell, Minoru released the protective shell.

First, the rubber strap of the mic device on his left wrist blew off.

Then a deep-crimson liquid sprayed everywhere.

However—

It wasn't blood from the enemy's body. The coat of living insects had liquefied instantly, this time of its own accord, and slipped out of Minoru's grasp.

Stinger's body was pushed upward as if riding on the surface of the diffusing shell.

That speed, however, wasn't enough to exceed the momentum of the burst.

As soon as the space between Minoru's arms closed, Stinger's right foot was caught there, and the Ruby's right leg was severed below the knee without any resistance.

This time, it was real blood that gushed out as Stinger was flung high into the air by the pressure of the burst—

And then stopped in midair.

A strange rustling sound reached Minoru's ears, no longer blocked by his protective shell. As soon as he recognized the source of the noise, he groaned.

"N...no way..."

Instead of returning to its original shape after liquefying itself, Stinger's coat had become a set of gigantic bat-like wings, flapping violently. In other words, the human being was flying.

Without the coat, Stinger's body was wrapped in tight clothes that resembled a bodysuit. It must have been made with the same ability, as the suit material was closed around the place where Stinger's lower right leg was severed, forming a spiral shape to prevent blood loss.

Hovering up above, Stinger stared down at Minoru from within the still-intact hood and gave a whisper. Despite the loud beating of the wings, the voice was as clear as if it had crept into his ear.

"...I'll be back for you soon."

With that statement, Stinger's artificial wings beat harder, carrying their owner straight up into the sky.

The roaring engines of an airplane descending from above covered the sound of Stinger's beating wings, and before long, the humanoid silhouette disappeared into the night sky.

Looking down, Minoru saw two objects lying on the asphalt at his feet. The syringe with a cracked cylinder and the severed right leg.

Which of these did they mean they'd be back for...? Minoru wondered absently.

"Would you hurry up and do something about this?"

Yumiko's voice brought Minoru back to his senses.

"Ah, r-right!"

Minoru hurried over to the spot where she was lying, roughly a meter away. The wireworm entangling her body had lost its tension now that it was out of Stinger's ability range, but its strength remained the same. Minoru tried to pull it with his hands at first, but of course, it didn't give an inch.

"There's a knife in the right inner pocket of my jacket."

"Right...o-oh, but, um..."

Minoru's left hand froze in the air. Because of the worms tied around her, Yumiko's biker jacket was pressed tight to her body. In order to get anything out of the inner pocket, he would have to do the impossible.

"Now's not the time to worry about that sort of thing. Hurry!"

She was right. Steadying himself, Minoru reached his hand into the gap between her black blazer and her jacket, searching for the inner pocket with his fingertips. Doing his best to ignore any sensations other than the firmness of the knife, he managed to pull it out, then breathed a sigh of relief.

Then, before Yumiko could scold him again, he quickly unfolded the collapsible blade and slid it under the wireworm. The worm resisted even the Aogami Super Steel blade for a while, but finally it frayed in the middle and broke. After Minoru repeated the same process two more times, the remaining restraints fell away, and Yumiko instantly rolled to her feet to pick up her fallen gun.

Zoom! An instant later, she accelerated over to the north side of the parking lot.

Stunned, Minoru followed her with his eyes, only to see that Liquidizer was no longer lying on the asphalt there. He looked around the parking lot, but the Ruby Eye in the sailor uniform was nowhere to be found. For her to move with a broken left arm and enough internal trauma to make her cough up blood must have taken considerable mental strength.

Using her ability again to return, Yumiko shook her head with a vexed expression.

"She's not anywhere nearby."

"Did she liquefy the ground and escape again?"

"I didn't see any traces of that. We'll have them put up a checkpoint at all the bridges that connect to this area... But first..."

This time, Yumiko simply walked across the lot, her riding shoes clacking on the asphalt.

She was heading toward the unconscious body of Trancer.

Since there hadn't been a Third Eye exodus from his body, he must still be alive, but he was completely unconscious. Yumiko stopped in front of his limp form, lifting the handgun in her right hand slightly.

After a moment's hesitation, Minoru called out to his partner's back. "...Yumiko..."

Apparently, that was enough to convey what he wanted to say to her.

A few seconds later, the Accelerator returned the handgun to her shoulder holster and took out a set of handcuffs from the case attached to her waist. She fit this over the wrists of the still-unconscious Trancer, then restrained his legs with a thick cable tie.

As Yumiko stood up to contact SFD Headquarters with her smartphone, Minoru watched her in silence. Fragmented memories of his exchange with Liquidizer echoed in the back of his brain.

That tiny little sphere is manipulating every one of us, without even realizing it...

Liquidizer had said something similar during the fight in Minami-Aoyama. That the Jet Eyes were being manipulated just like the Ruby Eyes.

It didn't seem that way to Minoru, as far as he could tell. However, he didn't believe that Liquidizer was lying, either. When she pleaded with him to save Trancer, there was real emotion reflected in her eyes.

As he looked up at the sky again, he thought he heard the far-off sound of a car engine, echoing like a sob.

8

Identified Ruby Eye Host No. 11, the boy who went by the code name Trancer, was still unconscious when he was loaded onto an ambulance to be sent to NCAM. DD, who arrived a few minutes after it was all over, rode in the ambulance with him at Yumiko's command (which she called a "request"), meaning that he was only on the scene for a total of less than five minutes.

Of course, he spent those minutes sniffing around for the scent of Ruby Eyes, but this only served to confirm that Liquidizer and Stinger were already beyond his detection range.

The parking lot of the cold-storage warehouse had been blocked off by the Metropolitan Police Department, and the forensics lab was already collecting samples. Because Stinger had scattered a huge amount of insects, it would probably take quite some time to collect all of them.

After reporting to Professor Riri Isa at headquarters, they sat side by side in the rear of the Delica D:5 that DD had parked just outside the lot, drinking the canned coffee they found inside the car.

The coffee was cold, of course; as he sipped on it, Minoru thought idly that if he were Trancer, perhaps he could heat it up again in an instant.

"…What's going to happen to him…to Trancer?"

After a moment, Yumiko shrugged lightly.

"If they go by the 3E case manual, it'll be the same as Igniter—they'll remove his Third Eye, and Chief Himi will erase his memories… probably."

"I see…"

If Trancer was no longer a Ruby Eye, would Liquidizer still think of him as someone she wanted to protect? Or perhaps…

"…I think there's a definite possibility that Liquidizer will come to the hospital to rescue Trancer before the Third Eye removal surgery."

Yumiko glanced at Minoru for a moment, then looked forward again.

"If she does, I imagine she'll certainly die this time. There aren't many guards on the first floor, but the 3E section on the eleventh floor is like a fortress… Personally, I think Stinger may have attacked you on the first floor partly in an attempt to take your key card…"

"Huh…? But that key card has fingerprint recognition, so unless I'm the one holding it…"

"Perhaps he would have cut off your fingers, too, then. But…his main goal was…"

"It was my blood."

Yumiko gave a small nod.

Apparently, the syringe Stinger dropped was an archaic glass model made for collecting blood. Minoru had no idea what Stinger would have done with his blood…or Trancer's, Yumiko's, and Liquidizer's…and he didn't want to know, either.

On top of that, it seemed like Stinger was trying to draw blood from the fallen Trancer's heart, not his arm. In that case, it was highly likely that Trancer would have died from the myocardial or arterial injuries. If Minoru and Yumiko hadn't followed him from Oomori, that might well have been exactly what happened, and Liquidizer could have fallen into Stinger's hands, too. So Minoru and Yumiko had saved not only Trancer's life but Liquidizer's as well…possibly, at least.

"…Why did Trancer run to a place like this…?"

Minoru looked up at the square cold-storage warehouse as he mumbled.

It wasn't a very deeply thought-out question, but Yumiko tilted her head thoughtfully, then finished her canned coffee and stood up.

"That's a good point. Perhaps there's something inside."

"Huh…?"

"Let's find out, shall we?"

With that, Yumiko trotted off briskly, and Minoru hurried after her.

Returning to the crime scene, Yumiko approached the detective from the Public Welfare Department. After a short conversation, he handed her something, and she walked back over to Minoru.

"What's that…?"

"The key to the warehouse, obviously. They haven't searched inside it yet, but he handed over the key quite easily when I said we wanted to ensure that there were no Ruby Eyes inside."

Easily, huh? He looked pretty sullen to me…

Keeping his thoughts to himself, Minoru followed Yumiko once again.

There was only one door in the wall of the warehouse that faced the parking lot, a rather old-looking one at that. When they unlocked the door, they found a place that looked like a break room, with a sofa, table, and TV. On the wall directly across from the entrance was a heavy door with a sign that said ENTRY STRICTLY PROHIBITED.

"…It's probably extremely cold in there, isn't it?"

"It's minus thirty degrees, they said. It'll be fine; I've done this before at an amusement park in Yokohama."

With that, Yumiko unhesitatingly opened the door. Inside was a narrow space that led to a set of double doors; when Yumiko closed the door behind them and opened these ones, a blast of cold air immediately stabbed at their skin.

"S-see? It's cold all right!"

The instant Minoru exclaimed that and inhaled through his nose instead of his mouth, his eyes widened.

Yumiko turned to him; she seemed to have noticed the same thing.

The scent of a Ruby Eye.

"Yumiko, what if there really is…?"

Minoru trailed off and shivered, and Yumiko gave the cryogenic air a few more sniffs before slowly shaking her head.

"It's not a fresh smell. I think…it's the trace of Ruby abilities that were used here."

"E-even if that's true, it could still be a trap…"

"There are employees in here all the time, right?"

She was right. Relaxing his shoulders a little, Minoru looked around again.

It wasn't quite as much a world of ice as he'd expected. The rows and rows of mobile racks stacked with countless cardboard boxes were frosted over, but the floor was dry concrete, so his feet didn't slip on the surface.

Following the faint smell, the pair advanced into the back of the warehouse.

About eighteen meters into the valley of racks, they abruptly met with a wall. There was nothing to the left and right but more boxes, which seemed to be full of frozen food—certainly nothing to worry about.

Just as Minoru was about to comment that there was nothing there, he heard a slight cracking sound at his feet.

Looking down, Minoru saw that one area of the floor was frosted over. The Ruby Eye scent grew a little stronger.

When he raised his eyes, he saw a concrete pillar sticking out from the front wall. It was noticeably covered in a thick layer of frosted-over ice.

"...The smell seems to be coming from this pillar."

With a whisper, Yumiko cautiously approached the pillar, wiping away the frost on the surface with the leather glove on her right hand.

The thick layer of transparent ice that covered the pillar was laid bare.

Inside, however...there was nothing.

All that could be seen through the ice was a blurry glimpse of the dark-stained concrete surface.

"There's nothing here..."

Minoru nodded in assent with Yumiko's murmur.

"Yeah... Although I do think the stain on the concrete looks a bit like a person...like a standing girl, maybe..."

"Stop that! This isn't some spirit photography."

Yumiko frowned, then jumped suddenly. Her smartphone was vibrating in her jacket pocket. Taking it out, she switched it to speakerphone mode.

"Yes, Azu here."

"Yukko? Is Mikkun there, too?"

It was the voice of Professor Riri Isa, who they'd reported to just a few minutes ago.

"Yes, he's right next to me."

"Okay. Both of you listen, then. We don't know yet whether it's related to this current case or not, but apparently, there was a previous incident in that cold-storage warehouse."

"An incident...? Was it related to Ruby Eyes?!"

Yumiko and Minoru looked around at once, but the Professor immediately responded.

"No, the incident occurred six years ago. A girl who was in the fourth grade at the time was found frozen to death in that very warehouse."

"A girl..."

"Frozen to death..."

Once again, the two of them looked back at the stain on the frozen pillar.

Unexpectedly, in the depths of Minoru's ears, Liquidizer's words played back again.

That boy has managed to stay himself all this time by hanging on to an illusion.

And it's probably his Third Eye that's showing him that illusion.

Minoru didn't know why he would remember those words at that moment. Once again, the Professor's voice came through the speaker.

"There had been reports at the local child guidance office that the girl was being abused... Her parents were interrogated, but the incident was ultimately deemed an accident. We're currently investigating whether she had any connection to Trancer, Liquidizer, or even Stinger."

"...Understood. We investigated inside the warehouse ourselves, but there didn't seem to be anything out of the ordinary."

"All right. Be careful on your way back."

After finishing the call and putting her smartphone away, Yumiko once again looked up at the pillar of ice.

However, she quickly turned away and spoke to Minoru.

"Let's get out of here. We're going to freeze if we hang out in this place much longer."

"...You're the one who said we should come in here in the first place...," Minoru muttered as he once again followed after Yumiko.

When they left the warehouse, the time was about eight o'clock.

Though he'd told Norie that he would be a little late, Minoru still felt guilty for missing dinner. He wanted to get home as soon as possible but couldn't quite bring himself to ask Yumiko to take him all the way from Ota Ward to Saitama.

As they walked through the parking lot, Minoru mumbled to himself.

"Maybe I really should buy a motorcycle..."

Immediately, Yumiko stopped short in front of him and turned around.

"Oh, really? Then I suppose I can come with you when you buy it. I recommend a supersport, of course, but it might be better for a beginner to start with something easier, like the street fighter type. There are a lot of good ones right now, even with a range under a million yen..."

Then she stopped abruptly.

"Wh-what's the matter?"

Yumiko blinked several times, then spoke with a strange expression.

"You know, I was thinking..."

"Yes...?"

"Isn't your twenty thousand, something hundred yen still in the Agusta's rear case...?"

"........."

Minoru froze, his mind rapidly retracing his memories of the last hours...

Then he slowly nodded three times.

After a moment, the two of them headed toward the exit of the parking lot, running with all their might.

The End